Room Below The World

K.E.W.

Published by White Quill Writings, 2024.

This is a work of fiction. Similarities to real people, places, or events are entirely coincidental.

ROOM BELOW THE WORLD

First edition. August 17, 2024.

ISBN: 979-8227048035

Written by K.E.W..

Also by K.E.W.

The Pineworth Chronicles
The Crossroads Of Duty
The Often Forgotten Hero
A Rookie's Journey
Secrets Among The Stones
1971

Standalone
The Pineworth Chronicles
Room Below The World

Table of Contents

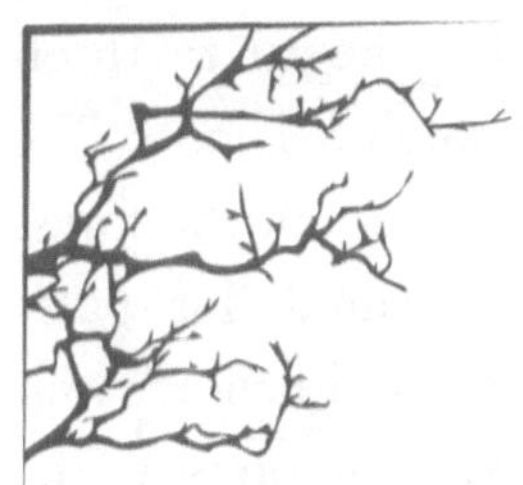

Prologue

The night hung heavy with an unnatural stillness, as Tyler Lawson slipped into the embrace of sleep. The sterile confines of the hotel room faded away, replaced by a dreamscape that teetered on the edge of the familiar and the unknown. He found himself standing in a dense, primeval forest, the trees towering above him with their twisted, gnarled branches, clawing at a sky painted with bruised and ominous hues.

The air was thick, laden with an oppressive fog that clung to his skin, seeping into his lungs with each breath. A profound silence surrounded him, broken only by the distant rustle of unseen creatures lurking in the shadows. An inexplicable dread began to gnaw at his senses, a sensation that something malevolent watched him from the darkness, just beyond his sight.

With a cautious step, Tyler began to walk, the ground beneath him uneven and treacherous. The path twisted and turned, leading him deeper into the heart of the forest. The trees seemed to close in around him, their branches forming a suffocating canopy that blotted out what little light remained. Each step he took seemed to draw him further into a labyrinth of despair, the path ahead obscured by the ever-thickening fog.

As he ventured deeper, a rhythmic pounding began to throb through the earth beneath his feet, resonating through his bones. The sound grew louder, more insistent, as if the very heart of the forest pulsed with a dark and ancient power. Tyler halted, his pulse quickening in time with the relentless beat. The ground beneath him trembled, the very earth seeming to shift and buckle in response to the unseen force.

Tyler's unease deepened, a cold sweat breaking out across his brow as the surrounding forest began to shift and twist. The trees leaned in closer, their branches reaching out like skeletal fingers, and the path became more treacherous with each step. His breath came in ragged gasps as he struggled to maintain his footing on the unstable ground, the oppressive atmosphere closing in around him.

Suddenly, the pounding ceased, and the forest fell into a deathly silence. The absence of sound was more terrifying than the noise had been, a void that seemed to swallow all light and hope. The air grew colder, the fog thickening until it was nearly impenetrable. Tyler felt the ground beneath him shift once more, the earth quaking as if alive, and he stumbled forward, trying to escape the unseen terror that pursued him.

But the path ahead was gone, swallowed by the shadows that pressed in from all sides. The forest had become a cage, its dark limbs imprisoning him in a web of despair. His heart pounded in his chest as he searched desperately for a way out, his mind racing with fear and confusion. The darkness loomed closer, a tide of malevolent force that threatened to engulf him completely.

In the distance, a faint light flickered, barely perceptible through the dense fog. Tyler's breath caught in his throat as he realized it was his only chance. With every ounce of strength he could muster, he broke into a run, the forest closing in behind him as he sprinted toward the distant glow. His legs burned with the effort, the rough ground tearing at his feet, but he pushed on, driven by a desperate need to escape the encroaching darkness.

The light grew brighter as he neared, a shroud of hope in the suffocating gloom. But just as he reached out to grasp it, the ground beneath him gave way, and he was plunged into darkness. The sensation of falling gripped him as the world around him dissolved into a void, the light extinguished as swiftly as it had appeared.

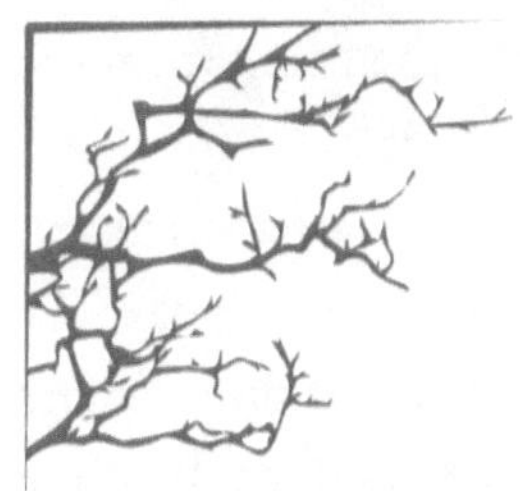

Chapter 1

A Morning Without End

TYLER LAWSON WOKE TO the soft murmur of the city coming to life outside his hotel window, feeling the weight of another long day ahead.

He squinted at the pale glow filtering into the room, feeling the weight of another long day ahead. The chirping of birds outside the window was a welcome contrast to the city's usual harshness, a reminder of the peaceful start to a day that would bring him closer to home.

He couldn't shake the dream he had. It lingered in his mind.

What could it mean? If dreams mean anything at all. He decided to put this thought behind him, besides, he was leaving soon. Back to his family that he misses so much.

Tyler stretched out his stiff muscles, savoring the brief quiet moment before the whirlwind of meetings and presentations began again. He rubbed his tired eyes and glanced at the framed photos on the nightstand—images of his family that had traveled with him for just such moments of homesickness. Jessica's radiant smile, Oliver's mischievous grin, and Grace's wide-eyed wonder seemed to beckon him from the glossy surfaces.

The aroma of freshly brewed coffee drifted into the room from the hotel's breakfast area, mixing with the faint scent of his own aftershave. Tyler could almost taste the rich, creamy warmth of a good cup of coffee, something he had come to depend on to start his day. He imagined the comforting ritual of his own kitchen at home, where Jessica would have brewed a pot, and the kids would be bustling around, chattering about their plans for the day.

As he got out of bed, the cool touch of the hotel floor against his feet was a stark contrast to the warm, soft rug at home. He padded over to the window, pushing aside the curtain to take in the view of the city slowly waking up. The skyline, bathed in the golden light, reminded him of the skyline back home, though the silhouettes of trees and rolling hills punctuated that one.

Tyler's mind wandered once more to his family, the ache of missing them more pronounced with each passing moment. He thought of Jessica's laugh, a sound he missed more than he realized, and the way Oliver and Grace's voices blended into a symphony of youthful energy. His heart yearned for the simple pleasure of their morning routines—sharing breakfast, helping with school projects, or just lounging together on a lazy weekend.

He imagined the warm embrace of Scout, their loyal dog, curling up at his feet as he drank his coffee. The thought of her wagging tail and the way she'd nuzzle against him filled him with a deep longing. The hotel room, though comfortable, felt sterile and impersonal compared to the warmth of home.

Tyler prepared for the day with a sense of eager anticipation. Each routine gesture—a quick shave, adjusting his tie, and packing his briefcase—was infused with the hope of soon returning to the life he cherished. The distant sound of a city awakening faded into the background as his thoughts were fully consumed by the anticipation of reuniting with his family.

He glanced at the clock and realized it was time to head out. With a final look at the photos from the nightstand, Tyler gave himself a silent pep talk, promising that this was one more step towards coming home.

As he left the hotel room, the crisp morning air greeted him, and he took a deep breath, savoring the fleeting sense of calm before the busy day ahead.

He picked up his phone, his fingers moving with practiced ease to dial Jessica's number. The familiar ringtone echoed faintly in the quiet hotel room before she answered.

"Hey, Jess," Tyler said, his voice carrying a hint of fatigue but also warmth. "It's me. I just wanted to let you know I'm heading home from the city."

"Tyler! That's great news!" Jessica's voice crackled with enthusiasm over the line. "We've missed you so much. How was the trip?"

"Busy, as usual," Tyler replied, his lips curling into a smile at the sound of her voice. "But everything went well. I'm looking forward to getting back. I can't wait to see you and the kids."

"We're all looking forward to it too," Jessica said. "Oliver's been asking about you every day, and Grace keeps drawing pictures to put on your desk when you get home. Scout's been a little restless, missing you."

Tyler chuckled aloud. "I'm sure she has. I've been missing all of you more than I thought possible. It's been too long."

"I know, sweetie," Jessica said, her voice softening. "We're counting down the hours. I've got a surprise planned for dinner, something special for your first night back."

"You're the best," Tyler said, his voice filled with genuine appreciation. "I'm really looking forward to it. I'll be home as soon as I can. Just wanted you to know."

"Safe travels, love. See you soon," Jessica replied, her tone full of affection.

"See you soon, I love you" Tyler echoed.

"I love you too," she replied.

He ended the call with a contented sigh, feeling a renewed sense of anticipation for the moment he would finally step through the door and back into the warmth of his family's embrace.

Tyler stepped out of the hotel, the brisk morning air waking him up a bit more. As he approached the curb, he spotted David leaning against their rental car, looking more worn out than usual. David's eyes were slightly red, and he rubbed his face as if trying to push away the lingering fatigue.

"Hey, David," Tyler called out, concern evident in his voice. "You look tired. Do you want me to drive?"

David straightened up and forced a smile. "I'm fine, Tyler. Just a rough night. Besides, you've got a long day ahead. I can handle the drive."

He did have a long day ahead. Before heading home he had to go into the office and talk to his boss about the business meetings over the past week.

Tyler hesitated, glancing at David's tired face. "You sure? I don't mind taking the wheel. It's a long trip, and we need to be safe."

David waved off the concern with a dismissive gesture. "I appreciate it, but I've got it covered. Let's just get on the road so we can get home sooner."

Tyler nodded reluctantly, tossing his bag into the back seat and sliding into the passenger seat. He still felt uneasy, but he trusted David's judgment. Settling into the seat, Tyler thought again of his family and the comfort of home waiting at the end of the journey.

As they pulled away from the hotel, Tyler glanced at David once more, hoping his coworker's exhaustion wouldn't be a problem. The engine's steady purr filled the car, and the city began to fade behind them as they started the long drive home.

As the car merged onto the highway, Tyler glanced out the window, watching the cityscape gradually give way to suburban sprawl and then to open countryside. The rhythmic sound of the tires on the road provided a soothing backdrop to their journey.

David broke the comfortable silence. "So, how's the family doing, Tyler?"

Tyler turned to look at him, a warm smile spreading across his face. "They're doing great, thanks for asking. Jessica's been keeping everything running smoothly at home. Oliver and Grace are growing up so fast, sometimes it feels like I'm missing so much."

David nodded, his eyes briefly meeting Tyler's before returning to the road. "I can imagine. It must be tough being away from them so often."

"It is," Tyler admitted, his voice tinged with a touch of sadness. "But it makes the time we do have together even more special. I can't wait to get back to them. Jessica told me she's planning a surprise dinner for my return. It's little things like that which make all the hard work worth it."

"Sounds awesome. Must be nice to have that kind of support." he retorted.

"It really is," Tyler said, his gaze turning wistful. "And Scout, our dog, she's probably been missing me too. The kids keep telling me how she waits by the door every evening."

"That's sweet," David replied. "It's great that you have such a loving home to go back to. Not everyone's that lucky."

Tyler nodded, feeling a swell of gratitude. "I know. I'm lucky to have them. It's the thought of seeing them again that's kept me going through this trip."

After a few minutes, Tyler turned to David. "What about you, David? How've you been holding up?"

David sighed, his shoulders sagging a bit. "I'm doing okay, I guess. Still haven't found the one yet."

Tyler gave him a sympathetic look. "I'm sorry to hear that. I know it's tough."

David shrugged, his eyes fixed on the road ahead. "Yeah, it's just hard to meet the right person, you know? Especially with all the traveling and work. It feels like there's never enough time."

Tyler nodded understandingly. "I get that. It can be hard to balance everything. But don't stop looking, David. She's out there somewhere."

David glanced over, appreciating the encouragement. "Thanks, Tyler. It's just frustrating sometimes. I see guys like you with a great family, and it makes me wonder if I'll ever have that."

"You will," Tyler said confidently. "It might take some time, but you'll find her. And when you do, all this waiting will make sense. Just keep your heart open."

David smiled faintly. "I hope you're right. It would be nice to have someone to come home to."

"You will," Tyler repeated.

Tyler looked out the window, watching as the trees flowed by, their green leaves a blur against the clear blue sky. The steady motion of the car and the gentle rustling of the leaves had a calming effect, lulling him into a sense of peace.

As the landscape changed from city to countryside, Tyler felt his eyelids grow heavy. The rhythm of the tires on the road and the warmth of the sun filtering through the window were making it harder to stay awake. He thought about home, the dinner Jessica was planning, and the excitement on Oliver and Grace's faces when he walked through the door.

The soothing sounds of the road and the hypnotic passing of trees became a gentle lullaby. Tyler's thoughts began to drift, his mind wandering from one happy memory to another. He could almost hear the laughter of his children, the loud bark of Scout, and the comforting murmur of Jessica's voice.

Before he knew it, his head nodded forward slightly, and he dozed off, the sights and sounds of the journey fading into the background as sleep took over.

Tyler was jolted awake by the sudden screech of the brakes. His eyes flew open, heart racing, as the car came to an abrupt stop. He glanced over at David, who looked both apologetic and sheepish.

"Sorry about that, Tyler," David said, his voice laced with exhaustion. "I just realized I really need a coffee. Didn't want to risk it any longer."

Tyler rubbed his eyes and nodded, still shaking off the remnants of his nap. "No problem, man. Better safe than sorry."

David guided the car off the highway and into the nearest gas station, pulling up next to a pump. The station was a small, nondescript place, but it had a welcoming glow that promised hot coffee and a quick break from the road.

As the car came to a halt, Tyler stretched and unbuckled his seatbelt. "I could use a stretch anyway," he said, opening the door and stepping out. The cool air hit his face, waking him up further.

David followed suit, heading towards the convenience store attached to the gas station. "I'll grab us some coffee. You want anything else?" he asked, looking back at Tyler.

"Just the coffee is fine," Tyler replied, running a hand through his hair and taking a deep breath. "Thanks, David."

David nodded and disappeared into the store, leaving Tyler to stretch his legs and take in the surroundings. The hum of the gas pumps and the occasional car passing by on the highway were the only sounds breaking the morning stillness.

Tyler looked around, the brief interruption a reminder of how far they still had to go. But it also made him appreciate the journey, the small moments of rest and conversation that made the trip more bearable.

A few minutes later, David emerged from the store, two steaming cups of coffee in hand. "Here you go," he said, handing one to Tyler. "Hopefully this will keep us going until we get home."

"Thanks," Tyler said, accepting the cup with a grateful nod. He took a sip, the hot liquid warming him from the inside. "Let's hit the road."

As they started back on the road, the steady sound of the tires filled the car once more. Tyler took a moment to appreciate the fresh cup of coffee in his hand, the warmth seeping through the cup and into his fingers. He pulled out his phone, deciding to send Jessica a quick update.

He typed out a brief message: "Halfway home."

A moment later, his phone buzzed with her reply: "Can't wait to see you! Drive safe. We love you."

Tyler smiled, pocketing his phone and taking another sip of coffee. The thought of his family waiting for him filled him with a renewed sense of determination to make it home safely.

David glanced over at Tyler. "Everything good?" he asked.

"Yeah," Tyler replied, nodding. "Jessica's excited. Kids too. It's good to be on the way back."

David gave a small smile. "I'm glad. Let's get you home to them."

The two men fell into a comfortable silence, the miles passing by steadily as they made their way down the highway. The landscape continued to shift, the familiar sights and sounds of the journey blending into a backdrop of anticipation and hope.

Tyler continued sipping his coffee, the warmth and caffeine slowly revitalizing him. He looked out the window, watching the other cars driving by. A minivan pulled up beside them, and he noticed a family inside, singing together and laughing. The sight brought a smile to his face and a pang of longing for his own family.

He thought to himself that he would talk to Jessica about taking a trip as soon as possible. It had been too long since they had spent quality time together away from the daily grind. A vacation would be perfect to reconnect and create more cherished memories with Oliver and Grace.

Tyler took another sip of his coffee, savoring the idea of a family trip. The image of the singing family stayed with him, a reminder of the joy and spontaneity he wanted to bring back into his own life. As they continued down the highway, the thought of planning a getaway filled him with excitement and a renewed sense of purpose.

Tyler closed his eyes, letting his thoughts drift to his family. He imagined Oliver and Grace's laughter echoing through the house, Jessica's warm smile greeting him at the door, and Scout's eager bark as she raced to meet him. The anticipation of wrapping his arms around them all filled him with a profound sense of peace.

Tyler continued to gaze out the window, the sight of the passing landscape blurring together. He took another sip of his coffee, savoring the warmth and comfort it brought. As he glanced over at David, he noticed his coworker blinking rapidly, trying to keep his eyes open.

"David, are you sure you don't want me to drive?" Tyler asked, concern etched in his voice. "You look really tired."

David shook his head, his grip tightening on the steering wheel. "I'm okay, really. Just waiting for the coffee to kick in. It's been a long trip, but I've got this."

Tyler watched him for a moment, his worry deepening. "Alright, but if you feel even a little bit off, let me know. It's not worth the risk."

Tyler settled back into his seat, trying to shake off the uneasy feeling that had settled in his gut. He took a deep breath, closing his eyes for a moment. His mind wandered back to thoughts of home, the familiar comfort of his family, and the plans he would make for their next adventure together.

David nodded, flashing a tired but appreciative smile. "I will, Tyler. Thanks."

Moments passed. Tyler closed his eyes to hear the music playing through the car.

Just then, a deafening bang shattered the tranquility. The car lurched violently, tires screeching against the asphalt. Tyler's eyes flew open, heart pounding in his chest. The world spun in a chaotic blur of motion and sound.

"David!" Tyler shouted, but his voice was drowned out by the roar of metal and glass being ripped apart.

In an instant, everything went black.

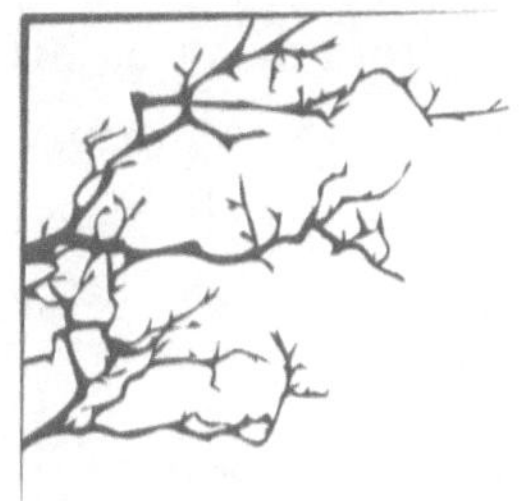

Chapter 2

Awakening

TYLER'S EYES FLUTTERED open to a dimly lit space that felt both strangely familiar and utterly alien. The room was small, it's only light was a feeble bulb hanging from the ceiling, casting a muted glow over everything. The air was still and heavy, filled with an unsettling silence.

He blinked several times, struggling to make sense of his surroundings. The walls were covered in a faded wallpaper with a pattern that seemed to ripple at the edges, almost as if it were alive. The furniture was sparse: a wooden desk with an old-fashioned lamp, a threadbare armchair, and a bed covered with a quilt that looked as though it had been pulled from a different era.

Tyler sat up slowly, his head spinning. The room felt like a snapshot from another time, but something was off—something he couldn't quite place. As he stood up, his legs felt weak, unsteady, as if he had just stepped out of a dream. He walked toward the door, only to find that it was locked. He twisted the handle, pulled, and shoved, but the door wouldn't budge.

A surge of panic gripped him. He backed away from the door, his heart pounding as he took in the details of the room. The wallpaper, the furniture, even the worn-out posters on the walls—they all looked strikingly familiar. It was as if he had been transported back to his childhood bedroom, a place he hadn't seen in years.

The walls seemed to close in on him, their edges appearing to inch closer with every heartbeat. Tyler's breathing quickened, his chest tightening as he sank to the floor. He clutched his chest, trying to steady his racing heart.

His breaths came in shallow, rapid gasps, each exhale mingling with the heavy air. The once-familiar space now felt suffocating and alien. The light flickered, casting eerie, shifting shadows that seemed to grow and writhe in the corners of his vision.

Tyler's mind raced, desperately trying to make sense of how he had ended up in this nightmarish replica of his childhood room. The air grew colder, and the walls seemed to pulse with a disquieting rhythm, as if the room itself were alive and watching him.

He felt a chill run down his spine, an unsettling shiver that had nothing to do with the temperature. The room, once a comforting relic of his past, had become a confounding, mysterious prison. The odd atmosphere and the distorted, shadowy corners made it clear that this was no ordinary space—it was something far more sinister, and there was no clear way out.

As Tyler struggled to calm his breathing and piece together the fragments of his disorientation, he was left with a single, overwhelming question: What was this place, and how could he escape it?

"Okay, Tyler, calm down," he murmured to himself, his voice trembling. "You can figure this out."

He took a deep breath, trying to steady his racing heart. The walls seemed to close in on him, their edges appearing to inch closer with every heartbeat. His breathing quickened, his chest tightening as he sank to the floor. He clutched his chest, trying to ground himself.

"Think," he told himself. "You've faced tough situations before. This is just another problem to solve."

He sat back down on the bed.

Tyler's breaths came in shallow, rapid gasps, mingling with the heavy air. The familiar space now felt suffocating and alien. The light flickered, casting eerie, shifting shadows that seemed to grow and writhe in the corners of his vision.

"Alright," he said aloud, forcing himself to focus. "You're in a room that looks like your old bedroom. It doesn't make sense, but that doesn't mean it's impossible to understand."

He rose unsteadily to his feet, his hands gripping the edge of the bed for support. The cold air pressed down on him, and the walls seemed to pulse with a disquieting rhythm.

"Just take it one step at a time," Tyler continued, speaking as much to reassure himself as to make sense of the situation. "Look for anything that might give you a clue. There has to be a reason for all this."

He moved slowly around the room, examining the furniture and the walls, his mind racing to piece together the fragments of his disorientation. The room, once a comforting relic of his past, had become a confounding, mysterious prison.

"Why am I here?" Tyler asked himself, his voice echoing in the dim, stifling space. He paced the small room, the question hanging in the air. The walls, adorned with faded wallpaper, seemed to press in on him, intensifying his sense of confinement.

He approached the locked door again, twisting the handle and pushing with all his might. "Kidnapped?" he considered aloud. "But why would they put me in a room that looks like my childhood bedroom? That doesn't add up."

Tyler's fingers traced the edges of the desk, feeling the worn wood beneath his fingertips. "If it's a kidnapping, who would go through all this trouble? Recreating my past? It's like they know exactly what would unsettle me."

He turned his gaze to the framed photograph on the desk. It was a picture of a young boy in front of a house that resembled his old family home. "Is this some kind of clue?" Tyler wondered, picking up the frame and studying it closely. "But what does it mean?"

He scanned the room. "Could it be a prank?" he asked, shaking his head. "No, this feels too real. If it were a prank, how did they get me here without me noticing?"

Tyler's eyes fell on the mirror, reflecting a pale, bewildered face. "Maybe it's an experiment or psychological test," he mused. "But who would do that, and why? This room doesn't fit that scenario either. It's too specific, too intimate."

He sat down heavily in the armchair, feeling its threadbare fabric beneath him. "Could it be a dream?" he questioned, looking around at the vivid details of the room. "No, everything feels too real—the quilt, the air, even the smell of the old wallpaper."

Tyler took a deep breath, trying to steady his racing heart. "Okay, if it's not kidnapping, prank, or dream, what else could it be? An alternate reality? A simulation? But why this room? Why recreate my childhood bedroom?"

He examined the old quilt on the bed, its frayed edges brushing against his fingers. "What if this is some kind of afterlife or another dimension? But why the specific room? What's the connection to my past?"

Tyler sank into the armchair, feeling the weight of the room press down on him. "Think logically," he told himself. "This room isn't just random. There has to be a reason behind it. Maybe understanding the room will lead me to understand why I'm here."

He began to methodically search the room, looking for anything that could provide a clue or hint about his situation. The eeriness made it clear that this was no ordinary space—it was something far more enigmatic.

Tyler's eyes roamed the room, desperate for any clue that might explain his bizarre situation. As he examined the worn wallpaper, the antique furniture, and the dusty desk, something else unusual caught his eye in the corner.

There, on a small, ornate stand, sat a vase with a few wilted flowers. These weren't any ordinary flowers; they were exotic and vibrant, clearly out of place in this otherwise familiar room. He knelt down for a closer look, noticing that the flowers' colors were strikingly vivid against the room's drab hues.

Carefully, Tyler lifted the vase, his gaze fixed on the flowers. "These definitely don't belong here," he muttered. "I don't remember ever having flowers like this in my room."

Inspecting the stand more closely, Tyler discovered a small, nearly hidden latch at its base. With cautious fingers, he pressed it. The hidden compartment opened with a quiet click, revealing a folded piece of paper inside.

Tyler's heart raced as he unfolded the paper. The note contained a single, handwritten phrase:

"Remember our special place."

His breath caught in his throat. The phrase was deeply personal—a term of endearment he and his wife, Jessica, had used since they were dating. It was a private reference to a cherished memory they had shared.

Tyler's mind raced. "This is something only Jessica and I would say," he realized, his pulse quickening. "Why would it be here?"

He looked around the room, trying to connect the message to his surroundings. "What does this mean in the context of all this?" he wondered aloud.

Just then, Tyler heard the faint sound of footsteps approaching outside the door. His pulse quickened, and he pressed his ear against the cold, wooden surface, trying to discern any distinct sounds. The footsteps were rhythmic and deliberate, growing closer with each step.

He shouted, "Hello?" His voice cracked with desperation. "Is someone out there? Please, help me!" He tried to make his voice as loud and clear as possible, hoping it would pierce through the heavy silence that filled the room.

The door, though solid and imposing, seemed to vibrate slightly with the intensity of his calls. Tyler could feel the vibrations against his palms as he pounded on the door with renewed energy. The sound of his own voice, echoing in the confined space, felt both reassuring and disheartening.

The faint aroma of old wood and dust filled the air, mingling with the musty scent of the room. Tyler's nose twitched at the smell, which seemed to grow stronger in the repulsive silence. He tried to ignore it, focusing instead on the hope that someone might come to his aid.

He listened intently as the footsteps outside the door came to a sudden halt. The sound of his own breathing, heavy and ragged, filled his ears. He strained to hear any further movement, but the only sound was the distant, indistinguishable hum of the house or building he was trapped in.

Tyler's eyes darted around the dimly lit room, desperately searching for any sign of change or movement. His skin tingled with a mix of hope and anxiety as he awaited a response. The door remained unchanged, its surface cold and unyielding against his touch.

He shouted again, his voice echoing more intensely in the small space. "Please, someone, help me! I'm trapped in here!" His throat was dry, the effort making his voice hoarse, but he continued to call out, determined not to give up hope.

The muffled sounds from outside—if there were any—remained elusive. Tyler's ears strained for any indication of movement or response, but all he could hear was the persistent silence and the beating of his own heart.

Tyler staggered back to the small twin bed, the worn quilt crumpling beneath him as he sank onto the edge. He buried his face in his hands, the weight of disbelief and frustration pressing down on him. His breaths came in ragged bursts, the quiet of the room now amplifying the turmoil in his mind.

The silence was shattered by a sudden, sharp knock at the door. Tyler's head snapped up, his heart pounding with renewed urgency. He stared at the door, his eyes wide with a mix of hope and apprehension.

"Who could it be?" he muttered, his voice trembling as he wiped his hands across his face, trying to clear the sweat and confusion. He listened intently, his ears straining to catch any additional sounds.

The knock came again, more insistent this time. Tyler's mind raced with possibilities. Was it someone who could help him, or was it another part of the elaborate trap? He stood up, his legs feeling unsteady beneath him, and approached the door cautiously.

He placed his hand on the doorknob, his fingers cold and clammy. The door seemed to mock him with its silence as he hesitated, his heart racing with every beat. "Hello? Is someone there?" he called out, his voice echoing in the confined space.

As Tyler stood in the doorway, the darkness of the hallway pressed against him, and the silence seemed almost palpable. Then, from the other side of the door, a deep, resonant voice cut through the stillness.

"Can I come in?"

The voice was steady and calm, yet it carried an undertone of authority that sent a shiver down Tyler's spine. He hesitated, his hand still gripping the doorknob. The voice sounded oddly familiar, but he couldn't place it.

Tyler's heart pounded in his chest. He glanced back into the room, the light from within casting long shadows across the floor. He turned his attention back to the hallway, trying to peer into the darkness beyond the open door.

"Who are you?" Tyler called out, his voice tinged with apprehension. "What do you want?"

The deep voice responded without hesitation. "I'm someone who can help you. But I need to come in to explain things properly."

Tyler took a cautious step back from the door, trying to weigh his options. The sound of the voice had an unsettling quality, and the request seemed both genuine and enigmatic. He could feel his pulse quickening as he grappled with the decision.

He glanced around the room, as if expecting something or someone to offer a sign. The silence around him felt heavy, making every second of indecision stretch longer.

"Alright," Tyler finally said, his voice trembling slightly. "You can come in."

As the door creaked open, the shadows in the hallway seemed to deepen, and a musty, old scent wafted into the room. The deep voice from the other side grew nearer, and Tyler's anticipation was mixed with unease.

An elderly man stepped into the room, his presence both commanding and oddly gentle. His long white beard flowed down to his chest, and his clothes were worn and outdated, as if he had emerged from a bygone era. The man's tattered brown coat and faded vest were a stark contrast to the modern world Tyler was familiar with.

The man moved with a deliberate, measured pace, his eyes holding a deep, weary wisdom. Tyler took an involuntary step back, his heart racing with a blend of fear and confusion.

"Who are you?" Tyler asked, his voice trembling. "What is this place? Why am I here?"

The elderly man stopped just inside the room, his gaze calm and steady. "I am someone who has been here for a long time," he said in a deep, resonant voice. "I'm here to help you understand what's happening."

Tyler's eyes flitted between the old-fashioned figure and the dimly lit room, trying to make sense of the surreal encounter. "Help me? I don't even know who you are. How can you help?"

The man took a slow step forward, his movements careful. "I understand this is overwhelming," he said gently. "But it is not what it seems. It's important that you listen."

Tyler's anxiety surged as he took another step back, his mind racing. "What do you mean? What is this place? How do you know about it?"

The elderly man's expression softened, his eyes reflecting compassion and understanding. "Everything will be explained in time. For now, you must trust that I am here to guide you through the process."

Tyler's hands clenched into fists, his breathing ragged. The room felt both constricting and oddly comforting with the man's presence. The stark contrast between the man's old-world appearance and the modern world Tyler had known was disorienting.

"Trust?" Tyler repeated, his voice tinged with skepticism. "How can I trust you when I don't even know who you are?"

The elderly man offered a faint, knowing smile as he settled into a chair. "Trust comes with time and understanding. For now, let's begin by talking. There's much you need to know, and I'll do my best to help you make sense of it all."

Tyler remained frozen in place, caught between fear and an unsettling curiosity. The elderly man's calm demeanor provided a strange contrast to Tyler's own turmoil, and as the man prepared to speak, Tyler had a feeling that the journey to unravel the mystery of his situation was just beginning.

The elderly man continued speaking, his voice steady and reassuring. "I know you have a lot of questions," he said, gesturing toward the small twin bed. "But sit down."

Tyler hesitated for a moment, his gaze shifting between the man and the bed. Finally, he sat down, the bed creaking gently beneath him. The man's eyes were kind but firm, as if he were both a guide and a guardian of sorts.

"Some of these questions you have do have answers," the man said, settling into a chair across from Tyler. "But I find you will cope better when you figure them out by yourself."

Tyler stared at him, a mixture of frustration and curiosity on his face. "You're saying you won't tell me what's going on?"

The elderly man nodded slowly. "That's right. I will help you navigate and offer guidance, but the answers you seek will come to you in their own time. Understanding will come from your own experiences and discoveries."

Tyler's mind was a whirlwind of confusion and anxiety. He wanted immediate answers, yet he felt the weight of the man's words. He took a deep breath, trying to steady himself. "So, what do I do now?"

The man's eyes softened with empathy. "For now, take your time to explore and understand your surroundings. Ask questions, observe, and listen. These rooms have their own rules and logic, and you will need to adapt to it."

"Rooms? As in more than one room?" Tyler asks.

The man shook his head confirming his question.

Tyler looked around the room, feeling a mixture of apprehension and curiosity. The old man's presence was both comforting and enigmatic. "Okay," Tyler said slowly. "I'll do my best."

The elderly man gave a small, approving nod. "That's all I ask. Remember, you're not alone in this. I'm here to assist you as you make your way through these revelations."

Tyler's eyes scanned the room again, his mind grappling with the unsettling familiarity of his surroundings. He turned back to the elderly man, a sense of disbelief in his voice. "How could my childhood room be recreated to look exactly the same? The room... it feels so real, but it's impossible."

The elderly man regarded Tyler with a patient, knowing look. "This room reflects what is important to you, Tyler. It is designed to evoke memories and emotions, providing a sense of comfort and familiarity in a situation that is otherwise disorienting."

Tyler shook his head, trying to grasp the concept. "But how is it even possible? Are we talking about some kind of advanced technology or...?"

The man raised a hand, his expression calm. "It's not about technology. It operates on principles that are beyond the conventional understanding of reality. It's not merely a room—it's a manifestation of your inner world and personal experiences."

Tyler frowned, struggling to understand. "So, you're saying this room is somehow a part of me?"

"Yes," the elderly man said, nodding. "It is a reflection of your memories and emotions. It will adapt to your sense of self, making it easier for you to process what is happening. The familiarity helps anchor you as you navigate this new existence."

Tyler's gaze drifted around the room, taking in the details—the faded wallpaper, the old wooden furniture, and the small knick-knacks that seemed so vividly real. "I suppose that makes some sense," he admitted. "But it still feels surreal."

"That's the nature of it," the man said.

"It bridges the gap between what you know and what you are beginning to understand. Your room is a starting point, a way to ease you into the process of discovery."

Tyler looked at the elderly man, his frustration evident. "Discovery for what? I don't understand what you're talking about. What am I supposed to be figuring out?"

The elderly man studied Tyler with a thoughtful expression. "Let's take a step back. What do you remember from before this moment? What was your life like?"

Tyler hesitated, trying to piece together the fragments of his memories. "I remember... I was on a business trip. I was with my coworker, David Turner. We were driving back home, and I was just thinking about my family—my wife, Jessica, and our kids, Oliver and Grace. I wanted to get home to them."

The elderly man nodded, encouragingly. "And what happened after that? What do you remember about the journey?"

Tyler looked up in the air as he concentrated, trying to recall the details. "We stopped at a gas station for coffee. David seemed really tired. I offered to drive, but he insisted he was fine. I was sitting in the car, looking out the window, thinking about how I wanted to plan a trip with my family. Then..."

His voice faltered, and he struggled to piece together the next moments. "Then there was a loud bang. Everything went black. I don't remember anything after that."

Tyler's mind raced with possibilities as he tried to make sense of the situation. He looked around the room again, taking in every detail, and then turned back to the elderly man. "Am I in some kind of treatment center or hospital? Is this all some kind of hallucination?"

The elderly man shook his head gently, his eyes filled with understanding. "No, Tyler, this is not a hospital or a treatment center. What you're experiencing is very real, though it may not fit into the conventional definitions you're used to."

Tyler's confusion deepened. "Then what is it? How can it be real if it feels like a dream or some kind of... alternate reality?"

The man took a slow breath, choosing his words carefully. "Where you are exists on a different plane of existence. It's a transition point, a bridge between the life you knew and the new reality you're now part of. It's designed to help you adjust and understand your new circumstances."

Tyler's heart pounded as he tried to wrap his mind around the explanation. "A different plane of existence? You're saying I'm... dead?"

Tyler's mind reeled as the elderly man's words sank in, each syllable echoing through him like a death knell. "You and your coworker, David, got in that car accident. You both didn't make it home.'" The sentence reverberated in his head, a relentless loop that crushed him with its finality.

He felt a cold sweat break out across his forehead, the chill contrasting sharply with the stifling warmth of the room. His skin prickled, goosebumps rising as if his body were rebelling against the truth. The taste of coffee, once comforting, now turned bitter in his mouth, a stark reminder of the last moments he shared with David.

The room, with its familiar scent of childhood—old wood, faint traces of his mother's perfume—became suffocating. The nostalgic aromas that once evoked warmth now felt like a cruel mockery of his reality. He stared at the faded wallpaper, its once soothing patterns now closing in on him, amplifying his sense of entrapment. The bed creaked beneath him, the sound magnified in the quiet space.

He buried his face in his hands, the rough texture of his palms grounding him in this nightmare. Tears welled up, hot and stinging, blurring his vision. His breath came in ragged gasps, each inhale a struggle against the crushing weight on his chest. "I'm dead," he whispered, the words tasting like ash in his mouth.

His thoughts turned to his family, a tidal wave of grief and regret crashing over him. He could almost hear Jessica's laughter, see Oliver's mischievous grin, and feel Grace's tiny hand in his. The memories, so vivid and tangible, were now unreachable, tainted by the knowledge that he would never hold them again.

Jessica. His rock, his partner. The thought of her waking up to an empty bed, receiving the news that he was gone—it shattered him. He could almost hear her sobs, the heartbreak that would echo through their home. The pain in his chest tightened, a physical ache that matched the emotional devastation.

Oliver and Grace. Their innocent faces flashed before him, the joy in their eyes when he walked through the door after a long day. He had promised them so many things—adventures, lessons, a lifetime of love and protection. The realization that he would never fulfill those promises was unbearable. He could see Oliver's confusion, and hear Grace's cries for her daddy. The thought of them growing up without him, facing the world without his guidance, was a torment beyond words.

The scent of flowers, fresh and out of place in the corner of the room, caught his attention. It was a cruel reminder of life continuing without him. The vibrant petals, so full of life, contrasted sharply with his own lifeless existence. He felt an overwhelming sense of loss, not just for himself but for the future that had been ripped away from his family.

The room's silence pressed in on him, a void filled with the echoes of everything he had lost. His senses, heightened by his emotional turmoil, made the ordinary details of the room unbearable. The sound of his own breathing was a painful reminder of his solitude. Every detail, every familiar object, became a symbol of what he could never return to.

Tyler sat there, overwhelmed by the crushing reality of his death. The weight of his loss, his regrets, and his unfulfilled promises pressed down on him, leaving him feeling hollow and broken. The world he knew, the life he cherished, was gone, and all that remained was the unbearable ache of what he had left behind.

The elderly man's expression was both gentle and firm. "Yes, Tyler. You and your coworker, David, passed away in that car accident. This is a form of afterlife, a place where you begin to come to terms with your new state of being."

The weight of the words hit Tyler like a physical blow, and he sank back onto the bed, his mind reeling. "Dead... but it feels so real. I can touch things, I can smell, I can hear..."

"That's because your senses are still active here," the man explained. "This room is designed to be familiar, to ease the transition and help you understand your new existence. It draws on your memories and emotions to create a space that feels real to you."

Tyler's thoughts raced as he tried to process the revelation. "So, this room, this place—it's all part of helping me understand that I'm no longer alive?"

. "It's a way to ground you, to help you cope with the transition. As you come to terms with your situation, you'll find more clarity and purpose in this new existence." The man replies.

Tyler nodded slowly, feeling a mixture of disbelief and acceptance. "I don't know how to process all of this, but I guess I don't have much choice, do I?"

The elderly man offered a small, encouraging smile. "Take it one step at a time, Tyler. There's no rush. You have all the time you need to understand and adjust."

Tyler's mind spun with the weight of his new reality. He looked up at the elderly man, desperate for answers, clinging to any shred of hope. "Is this... heaven?" he asked, his voice trembling with uncertainty.

The man's expression softened, and he sighed, as if he had faced this question many times before. "I'm not sure, Tyler. It can be whatever you choose to believe it is. Maybe it's heaven, if that's what you want it to be. Or perhaps it's a purgatory of sorts, a place of transition and reflection."

Tyler's heart sank further. "A purgatory? So, I'm stuck here, waiting for... what, exactly?"

The elderly man met his gaze with a mix of empathy and mystery. "That's something only you can determine. The realm will adapt to your needs and your beliefs. It's a reflection of your inner world, a space for you to come to terms with your past and your new existence."

Tyler felt a hollow ache in his chest. The thought of being in a limbo, neither here nor there, was almost too much to bear. He glanced around the room, his senses overwhelmed by the familiarity and strangeness of it all. The scent of old wood, the touch of the worn bedspread, the sight of his childhood treasures—all of it seemed like a cruel echo of a life that had slipped away.

"And what about my family?" Tyler's voice cracked. "Will I ever see them again?"

The man's eyes held a deep sadness. "They are still part of your journey, Tyler, even if you can't be with them in the same way. Where you are now allows you to observe, to remember, and to hold onto those connections in a different form."

Tyler's heart twisted with longing and despair. "So I just watch them from afar? I can't touch them, can't talk to them..."

The elderly man nodded slowly. "That is the nature of this existence. You can see their lives, feel their emotions, but you cannot interact with them directly. It's a different kind of presence, one that requires acceptance and patience."

Tyler felt tears sting his eyes again. The thought of being so close yet so far from his loved ones was a torment unlike any other. "I don't know if I can do this," he whispered, his voice breaking. "I don't know if I can bear it."

The elderly man placed a gentle hand on Tyler's shoulder, his eyes filled with compassion. "I'll leave you to figure out your new existence for now and mourn the life you've lost. It's a lot to take in, and you need time to process it all. I'll be back to check on you and help when you're ready."

Tyler nodded numbly, feeling the weight of the man's words settle over him. "What's your name?" he asked, his voice barely a whisper.

"Thomas Reed," the man replied, a faint smile touching his lips. "I'm here if you need me."

With that, Thomas turned and walked out of the room, closing the door behind him. Tyler stood there for a moment, the silence pressing in on him. He felt a hollow ache in his chest, the enormity of his situation sinking in.

He slowly turned back to the room, his eyes drifting to the corner where the flowers sat. The vibrant petals seemed out of place in this nostalgic recreation of his childhood sanctuary. Tyler walked over and knelt beside them, the faint scent of blossoms mixing with the musty smell of the old room. He reached out and touched a petal, its softness a stark contrast to the rough reality he now faced.

As he stared at the flowers, memories of his family flooded his mind—Jessica's laughter, Oliver's mischievous grin, Grace's innocent eyes. The thought of never holding them again, never hearing their voices, was an unbearable torment. The flowers, a symbol of life and beauty, now felt like a cruel reminder of everything he had lost.

Tears welled up in his eyes as he whispered to himself, "How do I go on from here?" The silence offered no answers, only the faint echo of his own grief. Tyler sank to the floor, his heart heavy with sorrow, staring at the flowers as the reality of his new existence began to take hold.

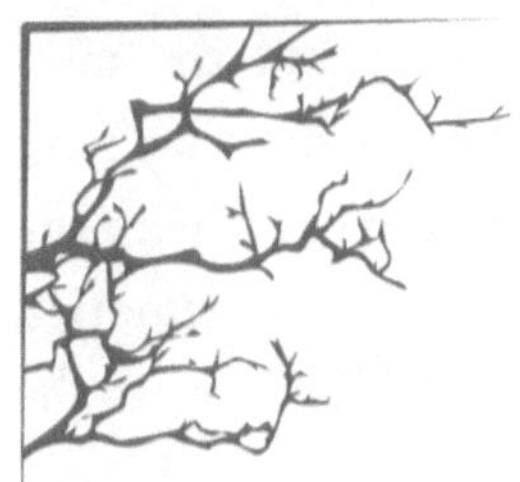

Chapter 3

What Went Wrong

Tyler sat on the edge of the small twin bed, staring blankly at the worn carpet beneath his feet. The weight of his new reality pressed heavily on his shoulders, and his mind replayed the events of that fateful day over and over again. He ran his fingers through his hair, the familiar gesture offering little comfort as he tried to piece together the puzzle of his demise.

"What went wrong?" he muttered to himself, the room's silence amplifying his words. He squeezed his eyes shut, desperate to block out the memories, but they flooded back with relentless clarity. The coffee stop, the brief conversation with David, the way the trees had blurred past the window as they drove. He should have insisted on driving. He should have seen how tired David was. He should have done something—anything—differently.

He could still see David blinking sleepily, hear his own voice asking if he should drive. He remembered David's reassuring but clearly fatigued response: "I'm fine, just waiting for the coffee to kick in." The regret gnawed at him, an insidious voice whispering that he could have prevented the crash if only he had been more insistent, more aware.

Tyler clenched his fists, the anger and frustration bubbling up inside him. "I should've driven," he whispered, the words a painful admission. He could almost feel the steering wheel beneath his hands, the control he would have had. If only he had been behind the wheel, they might have made it home safely.

The room, with its familiar scent of old wood and the faint perfume of flowers, seemed to close in on him. The weight of his guilt felt suffocating. He got up and began to pace, each step heavy with the burden of his thoughts. The walls, adorned with childhood memories, seemed to mock him. They stood as silent witnesses to his failure, to the moment his life was irrevocably changed.

He thought of Jessica, Oliver, and Grace, their faces vivid in his mind. He had promised them he would always come back, that he would always protect them. The thought of them mourning his loss, grappling with a future without him, was unbearable. "I let them down," he whispered, the pain in his voice cutting through the silence.

Tyler sat back down on the bed, his head in his hands. The regret was a heavy, unrelenting presence. "What could I have done differently?" he asked himself, though he knew the answer. He should have insisted on driving, should have taken control. But now, all he could do was replay the scene in his mind, a cruel loop that offered no solace, only a deeper sense of loss and helplessness.

He looked up at the flowers in the corner, their vibrant petals a stark contrast to his dark thoughts. They were a symbol of life continuing, even as his own had come to an abrupt end. The sight of them filled him with a bitter longing. He was trapped here, in this strange afterlife, left to grapple with his mistakes and the pain of what might have been.

As he sat there, lost in his thoughts, the door to the room remained closed, the silence pressing in on him. He was alone with his regrets, with the haunting question of what went wrong and the painful certainty that he would never find a way to make it right.

Tyler closed his eyes and took a deep breath, trying to calm the tumult of emotions within him. When he opened his eyes, the room had transformed. He was no longer in his childhood bedroom but in his bedroom with Jessica. Every detail was the same—the familiar scent of her perfume lingering in the air, the glow of the bedside lamp casting a warm light, the quilt they had picked out together spread across the bed.

He looked around, his gaze landing on their wedding photo hanging on the wall. He and Jessica, standing on the beach, smiling at each other with the ocean behind them. He remembered that day vividly—the way she had looked in her dress, the sound of the waves, the feel of her hand in his as they exchanged vows. A lump formed in his throat as he thought about how much he missed her, how much he longed to hold her again.

Tyler walked over to the photo and gently touched the frame, tracing the outline of their faces with his finger. "Jessica," he whispered, his voice breaking. The pain of their separation was a deep, aching wound that seemed impossible to heal. He missed everything about her—the way she laughed, the way she listened, the way she made him feel whole.

The room, with all its familiar details, felt like a cruel reminder of what he had lost. The quilt, the lamp, the photo—all of it spoke of a life that had been abruptly taken from him. He sat down on the edge of the bed, the mattress sinking slightly under his weight, and buried his face in his hands.

The scent of her perfume was a bittersweet comfort, a reminder of the closeness they had shared. He remembered the nights they had spent talking in this very room, planning their future, dreaming of the life they would build together. Now, those dreams felt like distant echoes, unreachable and lost.

"I miss you, Jess," he whispered into the quiet room, his heart heavy with sorrow. The emptiness around him was overwhelming, a constant reminder of the void her absence had created. He lay back on the bed, staring up at the ceiling, his mind filled with memories of their life together.

As he lay there, the room seemed to pulse with a strange energy, as if it were alive with the echoes of his past. The details of their shared life surrounded him, each one a testament to the love they had shared. The familiar sounds, smells, and sights brought a sense of comfort, but also a sharp pang of longing.

As Tyler lay on the bed, taking in every detail of the room that so perfectly mirrored his life with Jessica, he was jolted by a knock on the door. He sat up, heart pounding.

"Mr. Reed?" he called out, his voice trembling slightly.

"Yes, it's me," came the reply, the deep, reassuring voice of the elderly man. "May I come in?"

Tyler took a deep breath, trying to steady himself. "Yes, come in."

The door opened, and Thomas Reed entered the room. He looked around, taking in the transformation with a knowing smile. "Quite a change, isn't it?" he remarked, his eyes twinkling with curiosity. "How are you doing, Tyler?"

Tyler sighed, running a hand through his hair. "I don't know," he admitted. "One moment I'm in my childhood room, and now I'm here, in my bedroom with Jessica. It's overwhelming."

Thomas nodded, stepping further into the room. He glanced at the wedding photo on the wall, the quilt on the bed, the lamp casting its warm glow. "The room has a way of adapting," he said. "It's not just about where you are physically, but where you are emotionally."

Tyler looked up at the old man, searching for answers in his lined face. "Why does it do that? Why does it change?"

Thomas took a seat in the chair by the window, his gaze thoughtful. "It reflects your memories, your desires, your regrets. It's part of your journey to understand what's happened, to come to terms with it."

Tyler nodded slowly, the weight of his new reality settling over him once again. "I miss her so much," he said quietly, his voice filled with pain. "I miss all of them."

Thomas sat next to Tyler on the bed, his expression softening with empathy as he looked at Tyler. "Let me tell you a story," he began, his voice gentle. "Maybe it will help."

Tyler sat up a bit straighter, curiosity piqued. "Okay," he said quietly, ready to listen.

Thomas took a deep breath, his eyes distant as he recalled the memories. "I died in my bed, surrounded by my family. It was a peaceful passing, as far as those things go. My children, grandchildren, and even some great-grandchildren were there, holding my hands, speaking words of comfort."

He paused, his eyes meeting Tyler's. "I know you didn't have that. Your death was sudden, unexpected. But the feeling of loss, that ache in your heart, it's something we all share."

Tyler swallowed hard, the image of Thomas's peaceful death contrasting sharply with his own experience. "What happened to you?" he asked, needing to know more.

Thomas leaned forward, his voice steady and warm. "I was an old man, Tyler. I'd lived a long life. Seen many things, experienced joy and sorrow in equal measure. When my time came, I was ready. But even then, the thought of leaving my loved ones behind was painful. The separation, it's always hard, no matter how it happens."

Tyler nodded, feeling a connection with the old man's words. "I didn't get to say goodbye," he whispered, the regret heavy in his voice.

Thomas sighed, a deep, understanding sound. "I know, son. That's a burden many here carry. The abruptness, the lack of closure—it's a cruel reality. But you mustn't let it consume you. You still have your memories, your love for them. That's something no one can take away."

Tyler looked down at his hands, the reality of his situation sinking deeper. "It just feels so unfair," he said, his voice trembling.

Thomas reached out, placing a reassuring hand on Tyler's shoulder. "It does. And it is. But you have to find a way to live with it, to honor the life you had and the people you loved. It won't be easy, but it's the path we all must walk here."

Tyler took a deep breath, trying to absorb the wisdom in Thomas's words. "Thank you," he said, gratitude and sorrow mingling in his voice.

Thomas gave a small, encouraging smile. "You're welcome, Tyler. Remember, you're not alone. We're all in this together, figuring it out as we go. And I'll be here, whenever you need to talk."

Tyler nodded, feeling a glimmer of hope amidst the overwhelming sense of loss. "I appreciate that, Mr. Reed."

Tyler sat in silence for a moment, absorbing Thomas's words. He hesitated before speaking, uncertainty evident in his eyes. "Thomas, can I ask you something?"

Thomas paused at the door, turning back to face Tyler. "Of course. Ask anything you need."

Tyler took a deep breath, the question weighing heavily on his mind. "How come you can come to the room, but when I try to open the door, I can't leave?"

Thomas's expression grew thoughtful, a hint of sadness in his eyes. He walked back into the room, pulling the chair closer to Tyler's bed before sitting down. "That's a complex question, Tyler. The answer isn't straightforward."

Tyler leaned forward, eager to understand. "What do you mean?"

Thomas sighed, choosing his words carefully. "For some reason or another, you won't allow yourself to leave this room. Something within you is unsettled, preventing you from moving on. This place, it reflects our inner state. Some people stay in their rooms because they can't face what's outside. Their rooms can be beautiful, like this one, or they can be like cells, depending on their guilt, regrets, or unresolved issues."

Tyler frowned, confusion and frustration mingling in his mind. "So, you're saying it's my own mind keeping me here?"

Thomas nodded slowly. "In a way, yes. The door isn't locked by any physical means. It's your own feelings, your own sense of unfinished business that's keeping you confined. You need to confront whatever it is that's holding you back."

Tyler looked around the room, taking in every detail—the wedding photo, the quilt, the scent of Jessica's perfume. "I just don't understand. How do I confront something when I don't even know what it is?"

Thomas smiled gently, a reassuring presence in the midst of Tyler's turmoil. "That's part of your journey here. To figure out what it is that's keeping you from moving forward. It might take time, and it might be painful, but it's necessary."

Tyler nodded, though the confusion still lingered. "And what about you? Why can you come and go?"

Thomas's eyes widened with understanding. "I've been here a long time, Tyler. I've had my own struggles, my own barriers to overcome. But over the years, I've come to terms with my life and my death. It's a process, one that you'll go through as well."

Tyler sighed, the weight of Thomas's words pressing down on him. "I guess I have a lot to figure out, don't I?"

Thomas stood up, patting Tyler's shoulder gently. "You do. But remember, you're not alone. We're all here, facing our own battles. And you have time to work through it."

Tyler's frustration bubbled over, and he shook his head vehemently. "I don't have time, Thomas. I want to see my family. I can't waste time here."

Thomas paused, his hand still on the doorknob, and turned to face Tyler fully. His eyes held a mixture of empathy and understanding. "I know it's hard to accept, Tyler. But rushing through this process won't help. There are things you need to face, things you need to understand about yourself and your life."

Tyler stood up, pacing the room, his agitation evident in his every movement. "But my family needs me. I can't just stay locked up in this room while they're out there, missing me, mourning me."

Thomas nodded slowly, acknowledging Tyler's pain. "Your love for them is strong, and that's why this is so difficult. But this place, it's not bound by time in the same way the world is. You have to trust that your journey here is important for you and for them."

Tyler stopped and turned to Thomas, desperation in his eyes. "I just want to hold them again, to tell them I love them. Isn't there any way?"

Thomas's expression softened. "I can't give you all the answers, Tyler. But I can tell you that many here have felt as you do. It's a process, and it takes time and reflection. Your family will always be a part of you, and you will always be a part of them. But you need to come to terms with your own situation before you can find any peace."

Tyler clenched his fists, feeling the weight of his helplessness. "It's just so unfair," he whispered.

Thomas stepped closer, placing a comforting hand on Tyler's shoulder. "I know it feels that way now. But you're stronger than you realize. Take this time to understand yourself, to find out what's holding you here. It's the only way forward."

Tyler sighed, the fight draining out of him for the moment. "I'll try," he said quietly, his voice filled with a mix of resignation and determination.

Thomas stood up, his movements slow and deliberate. As he reached the door, he turned back to Tyler, a thoughtful expression on his face. With a small, reassuring smile, he said, "You know, sometimes things work themselves out anyway."

He gave Tyler a gentle nod, then opened the door and stepped out, leaving Tyler alone with his thoughts. The door closed behind him, the sound echoing in the quiet room. Tyler sat back down on the bed, turning over Thomas's words in his mind. Despite his frustration and uncertainty, the old man's smile lingered in his thoughts, bringing a glimmer of reassurance to his otherwise troubled heart.

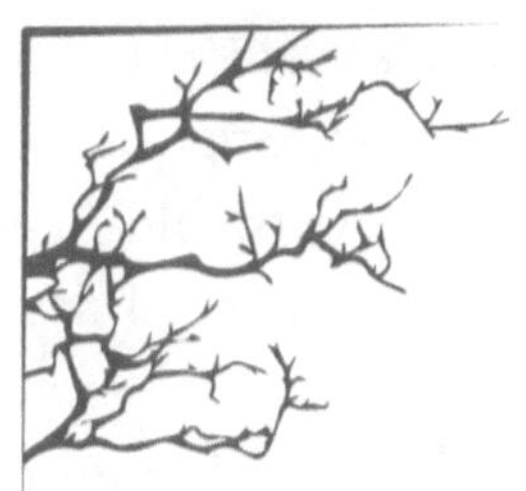

Chapter 4

The Silent Visit

Tyler paced back and forth in the small room, his thoughts a chaotic swirl of questions and frustrations. The creak of the door opening behind him broke his trance. He spun around, his heart racing, and was met with the sound of familiar voices—his family's voices.

"Mommy, are we here to visit Daddy?" Oliver's small, innocent voice echoed in the room, tugging at Tyler's heartstrings.

Tyler's breath caught in his throat as he watched the door slowly open wider. His wife, Jessica, stepped inside, holding a bouquet of fresh flowers. Behind her, Oliver and Grace followed, their little hands clutching each other. They couldn't see him, but to Tyler, they were right there in the room with him.

Jessica knelt down by the corner of the room, placing the flowers gently on the ground. "We miss you so much, Tyler," she whispered, her voice trembling with emotion. Oliver and Grace stood silently beside her, their eyes wide and solemn.

Tyler's chest tightened as he watched them, his family so close yet so far. The flowers, just like the ones he had found earlier, appeared in the corner of his room as if by some unseen force. It was a heartbreaking reminder of the distance that now separated him from the people he loved most.

Tyler stood frozen in the middle of the room, his eyes locked on Jessica as she knelt by the corner, speaking softly as if he were right there beside her. The air felt thick with the scent of fresh flowers, mingling with the faint aroma of her perfume—an all too familiar smell that tugged at his heart.

"Oliver is doing so well in school, Ty," Jessica whispered, her voice cracking with emotion. "He got an A on his last math test. You'd be so proud of him." She wiped a tear from her cheek, her hand trembling as she continued. "And Grace... she's been loving basketball. She's got your competitive spirit, always pushing herself harder."

Tyler's heart ached as he listened to her words, the warmth in her voice contrasting with the cold, sterile feel of the room. He could see every detail of her face—the way her eyes, usually so bright, were now clouded with sadness. Each tear that rolled down her cheek seemed to glisten in the dim light, a silent testament to her grief.

He could hear the quiet sniffles of his children, Oliver's quiet attempts to be brave for his mom, and Grace's tiny sobs that broke through her usual tough exterior. The sound of Jessica's voice, tender and full of love, was like a balm to his soul, even as it tore at the edges of his heart.

Tyler's fingers tingle with the desperate need to reach out and touch them, to wipe away their tears and tell them he was still here, still with them. But the icy chill of his own reality reminded him that he couldn't—his hand passed through the air, unable to connect with the warmth of their presence.

As he watched Jessica, her shoulders shaking with the weight of her emotions, Tyler felt a wave of both sorrow and comfort wash over him. Sorrow because he couldn't hold her, couldn't tell her how much he missed them too. But there was comfort in her words, in the love she still carried for him, a love that transcended the boundaries of life and death.

The room, though cold and silent, seemed to pulse with the lingering essence of their connection. Tyler breathed in deeply, catching the faint scent of home that clung to Jessica's clothes, the smell of fresh laundry mixed with the familiar hint of lavender. It filled him with a bittersweet longing, but also with a sense of peace.

Tyler, feeling the overwhelming weight of his emotions, took a tentative step forward. He reached out toward Jessica, his voice trembling with desperation. "What about you?" he said, his words thick with sorrow. "How are you, Jess? I'm so sorry I left you. I never wanted to leave you."

He knew she couldn't hear him, that his voice was just a whisper in the void between life and death, but he had to say it. He had to try. His eyes, stinging with unshed tears, fixed on her face, searching for any sign that she might sense his presence.

Jessica remained still, her tears falling gingerly onto the flowers she had placed by the corner. She didn't react to his words, didn't look up or pause as she continued to talk to the children. But Tyler's heart refused to give up. He spoke again, more urgently this time, the pain in his chest almost unbearable.

"Jess, I'm so sorry," he repeated, his voice breaking. "I should have been there for you, for the kids. I never wanted to leave you alone."

But the room remained silent, except for the faint echoes of his family's voices. It was as if his words had been swallowed by the very walls around him, unable to reach the one person he needed to hear them. Tyler's shoulders slumped in defeat, his heart heavy with regret.

As Tyler stood in the room, his heart aching with the weight of unspoken words, he suddenly froze. Jessica, her voice trembling yet strong, spoke as if she had heard him.

"Don't worry about me," she said, her words carrying a warmth that seemed to reach across the divide between them. "I can take care of the kids. We miss you every day, but we'll be okay. I promise."

Tyler felt a rush of emotion flooding through him. Could she somehow sense him, feel his presence in the room? His eyes welled up with tears as he listened to her speak, each word a balm to his wounded soul.

"I'll always miss you, Tyler," Jessica continued, her voice cracking slightly. "You are the love of my life, and I'll carry that with me forever."

As Jessica gently urged the children to say their goodbyes, Tyler watched helplessly, his heart breaking with each word. Grace whispered her farewell, her small voice trembling, but it was Oliver who caused Tyler to hit the breaking point.

Just as they turned to leave, Oliver paused, glancing back toward the room with a look of pure, innocent longing. His eyes seemed to search the space, as if he could sense something, someone. And then, with a voice low but sure, he said, "I miss you, Daddy."

Tyler's world crumbled in that instant. Tears streamed down his face, blurring his vision as he reached out, desperate to hold his son, to wrap him in his arms and never let go. The need to protect, to comfort, surged through him, a primal force that tore at his very soul. But his arms passed through the air, empty, powerless.

He watched in anguish as his family disappeared through the door, the finality of the closing echoing in his heart. When the door shut, it was like the last thread connecting him to the life he knew had been severed.

A flood of emotions surged within him—grief, regret, an unbearable ache of loss. He felt crushed by the weight of his helplessness, his inability to be there for the ones he loved most. Anguish twisted inside him, and he was consumed by the desperate, futile wish to turn back time, to be with them again, to hold them just once more.

But along with the sorrow, there was also a tender, heartbreaking love—a love so deep it defied the boundaries of life and death. Tyler sank to the floor, his body wracked with sobs, the tears falling freely as the reality of his situation closed in around him. The room felt colder, emptier, a silent reminder of all he had lost and the void that now stretched out before him.

Tyler sat slumped on the floor, his tears gradually subsiding into a numb silence, when he heard the familiar, gentle knock at the door. He looked up, his voice hoarse but steady, "Come in."

The door creaked open, and Thomas stepped into the room, his presence like a reassuring light in the midst of Tyler's darkness. The old man's eyes were filled with a deep, compassionate understanding as he surveyed the scene—Tyler's tear-streaked face, the lingering scent of flowers, the empty space where his family had been.

Thomas took a slow, measured step toward Tyler and spoke in a voice both gentle and firm, "I saw your family just now. It must be incredibly difficult. If there's anything I can do to help you through this, please let me know."

Tyler looked up at Thomas, his face still wet with tears, his heart heavy with grief and longing. He could barely find the words to express the depth of his sorrow. But there was something comforting about Thomas's offer, a small flicker of hope amidst the overwhelming darkness.

"Thank you," Tyler managed to say, his voice cracking. "I... I don't even know what to ask for right now. I just—"

He struggled to find the right words, the ache in his chest making it hard to speak. Thomas nodded, his gaze filled with empathy. "Sometimes just having someone to listen to can make a difference. You don't have to go through this alone."

Tyler nodded, grateful for the offer of companionship in his time of need. He took a deep breath, trying to compose himself, and allowed Thomas's presence to be a small comfort in the midst of his pain.

Tyler wiped his eyes with the back of his hand, trying to steady his breath as he looked up at Thomas. "Tell me about what it's like," he asked, his voice raw. "What's it like being able to walk out the door? Is it better or worse?"

Thomas took a moment, his eyes reflecting a deep, distant sadness. He walked over to a nearby chair and sat down, his movements slow and deliberate as if choosing his words with care.

"It's different for everyone," Thomas began, his voice carrying the weight of experience. "For some, stepping out of the room is a way to find solace, to see the world one last time, even if it's through a veil. For others, it's a painful reminder of what they've lost and what they can no longer touch or change."

He paused, his gaze drifting as if seeing beyond the walls of the room. "You see, walking out doesn't change the fact that you're still bound by your own emotions and regrets. It's like being a ghost of sorts—able to observe but never fully interact. You see the lives you left behind, and it can be both beautiful and heartbreaking."

Thomas looked back at Tyler, his eyes compassionate but weary. "For me, it's been a mix. Sometimes it was comforting to see my family again, to watch over them, to make sure they're alright. But it also hurts, when I saw them live their lives without me, knowing that I couldn't be a part of it. It's a bittersweet existence."

He leaned forward slightly, his voice softer. "The freedom to walk out of the room might offer some solace, but it also brings its own set of challenges. It's about finding a balance, coming to terms with the new reality, and accepting that some things are beyond our control."

Tyler listened intently, absorbing Thomas's words. The idea of leaving the room, of witnessing life from the outside, was both intriguing and daunting. He felt a mix of hope and apprehension, uncertain of what it would mean for him personally.

Thomas offered a gentle smile. "If you decide to take that step, remember to be gentle with yourself. It's not an easy path, but it might help you find some answers and peace."

As Thomas finished speaking, the room was momentarily quiet, the only sounds being the rustle of fabric and the hum of Tyler's thoughts. Suddenly, faint but unmistakable voices drifted into the room, breaking the silence.

"Mom? Dad?"

Tyler's heart leaped at the sound. His head snapped toward the door, his pulse quickening as he strained to hear more clearly.

Thomas, observing Tyler's reaction, placed a reassuring hand on his shoulder. "I'll leave you for now," he said, his eyes filled with understanding. "You need this time with your visitors. I'll come back later to check on you."

With that, Thomas gave Tyler one last empathetic look and walked towards the door. As he opened it, the voices became clearer, their sounds more distinct.

"Mom? Dad? Where are you?"

Tyler's heart raced as the door slowly closed behind Thomas. The room seemed to hold its breath in anticipation. Tyler stood frozen, his emotions a tangled mess of excitement and fear, as he prepared to face whoever was about to enter.

The door creaked open just a fraction, and Tyler could see the outlines of figures starting to come through. His breaths came in shallow, uneven gasps, a mixture of hope and anxiety welling up inside him as he braced himself for the sight of his family.

The door creaked open, and Tyler's breath caught in his throat as his mother stepped into the room. She wore a somber black dress, and in her hands, she carried a bouquet of delicate flowers. Her face was lined with sadness, her eyes glistening with unshed tears.

Without a word, she walked to the corner of the room where the other flowers had been placed, gently laying down her own bouquet beside them. The flowers were a mix of muted colors—lilies, roses, and forget-me-nots—each one a symbol of love and remembrance.

For a moment, she stood there in silence, her shoulders slightly hunched, as if gathering her thoughts. Tyler watched her, his heart aching at the sight of his mother in mourning.

Finally, she spoke, her voice quivering and filled with emotion. "I miss you so much, Tyler," she said, her words trembling. "It's been so hard without you here. I've been trying to look after Jessica and the kids as best as I can. Jessica has been incredibly strong through all of this, and the kids... they're so smart and brave. They miss you too, every single day."

She paused, wiping a tear from her cheek. "It's amazing how resilient they've been. Jessica's been holding everything together, and I can see how much she's been struggling, but she's doing her best for them. They're growing up so quickly. Oliver is doing so well in school, and Grace has really taken to basketball. They're thriving, but they still need you."

Tyler's heart ached with every word. He felt a surge of love and sadness, knowing how much his absence had affected his family. He wanted to reach out, to comfort his mother, to tell her he was there for her too, but the distance between them was as real as ever.

His mother's voice was a soothing balm amid his pain, but it also deepened his sorrow, reminding him of everything he had lost.

As Tyler's mother continued to speak, the door creaked open once more, and his father stepped into the room. His presence was a stark contrast to his wife's quiet demeanor. He wore a dark suit, his face etched with a deep, unspoken sorrow.

He moved slowly toward his wife, his steps heavy with the weight of his grief. Standing behind her, he placed his hands gently on her shoulders, offering a silent but powerful gesture of support and comfort. The touch was tender, yet it conveyed the depth of his own anguish.

His father's face was lined with the kind of pain that words could not adequately express. The lines around his eyes and the downturn of his mouth spoke volumes about the heartache he was feeling. Although he remained silent, the intensity of his emotions was palpable, more profound than any words could convey.

Tyler watched his father, feeling a swell of emotion rise within him. The sight of his father's hands on his mother's shoulders, the way he seemed to draw strength from her, was a poignant reminder of the love and unity that had always been a cornerstone of his family.

His father's eyes met Tyler's, and in that moment, there was an unspoken connection between them—a shared understanding of loss and the enduring bond of family. The pain in his father's gaze was a mirror of Tyler's own sorrow, a reflection of the void left by his absence.

Tyler watched as his father gently turned his mother around, guiding her toward the door. The shuffle of their steps echoed in the room, a stark contrast to the silence that had enveloped them. As they moved toward the exit, Tyler's heart ached with every step they took away from him.

Just before they reached the door, his father paused, turning slightly to cast one final, fleeting look back at Tyler. A single tear traced a path down his father's weathered cheek, shimmering in the soft light of the room. The tear seemed to capture the essence of all the unspoken words, the grief that words alone could not convey.

In that brief moment, Tyler felt a profound understanding pass between them. His father's silent gesture spoke volumes—an acknowledgment of the deep pain they all shared and a reminder of the strength his father had to muster in the face of their collective sorrow.

Tyler felt a swell of gratitude for that fleeting look. It was a small but powerful acknowledgment of the love and connection that still bound them together, despite the chasm of death. The silent exchange was both a comfort and a poignant reminder of the family he had left behind.

As his parents disappeared through the door, Tyler was left with the echo of their presence and the lingering warmth of their love. The room seemed to settle into a quieter, more reflective silence, punctuated only by the faint memory of their visit.

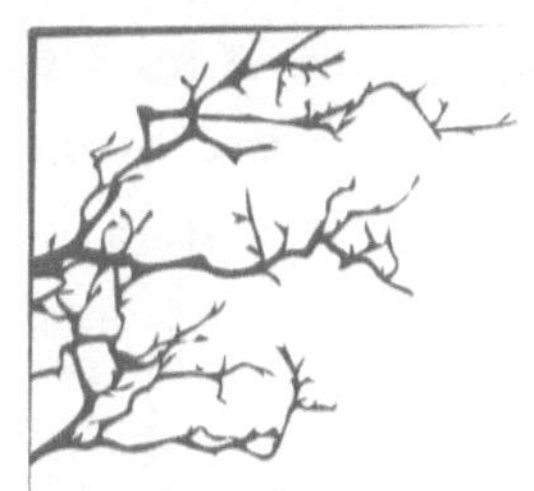

Chapter 5

Echoes of Regret

As Tyler grappled with the weight of his emotions, the comforting familiarity of his bedroom began to dissolve. The room around him started to shift in subtle ways. The warm, cozy space that once held his cherished memories with Jessica began to blur and melt away.

The edges of the room softened, and the once-intimate space transformed into something more clinical. The comfy bed and the inviting textures of his bedroom were replaced by the rigid lines of a stark office environment. The walls that had been adorned with personal touches and family photos now turned into cold, metal panels.

The room's colors shifted from warm hues to harsh, sterile whites and grays. The comforting softness of the bed evaporated, replaced by the hard, unyielding surface of an office desk that appeared in the center of the room. The once-familiar scent of home was replaced by the sharp, acrid odor of printer ink and office supplies.

The once plush carpet gave way to the cold, hard tile of an office floor. The gentle, calming light that had filtered through the bedroom curtains was replaced by the harsh, fluorescent glow of ceiling lights. The space felt impersonal with its sterile, corporate feel.

The personal touches of Tyler's bedroom vanished, replaced by the clutter of an office—stacks of papers, a cluttered desk, and framed certificates lined the walls. The comfortable armchair and bedside table were now an ergonomic office chair and a cluttered desk covered in reports and files.

As Tyler took in the change, the comforting presence of his wife and the intimate warmth of their shared space were replaced by the cold, detached reality of his work environment. The transition from the personal to the professional was jarring, leaving him with a profound sense of dislocation.

Tyler paced around the newly transformed office, his steps echoing off the cold, hard tile. The room, now stark and impersonal, was a tangible reminder of the life he had left behind—the work, the stress, the never-ending grind. Yet, as he walked, his mind fixated on one single source of torment: David.

The office, with its cluttered desk and piles of paperwork, felt cruel. Each file, each report, was a reminder of the responsibilities Tyler had once shouldered, and each one served as a backdrop for his simmering resentment. The sterile environment only seemed to amplify his feelings of anger and betrayal.

Why hadn't David said anything about being tired? The thought gnawed at him. Tyler's mind replayed their last conversation—David insisting he was fine, brushing off Tyler's offer to drive. The frustration welled up inside him. The accident, the loss, everything could have been avoided if David had just admitted his fatigue.

Tyler's gaze fell on a framed certificate on the wall, its gold trim glinting under the harsh fluorescent light. It was a stark contrast to the warmth of his home, a symbol of the achievements and the relentless pursuit of success that had defined his career. It seemed almost mocking now, a reminder of what had been taken from him.

The office's sterile air seemed to choke him as he struggled to breathe, his resentment building with each step. He clenched his fists, trying to steady himself, but the anger remained. David had taken more than just his chance to live; he had taken away his family, his future, his very sense of self. Tyler felt as if he was suffocating under the weight of his unresolved anger and loss.

As he continued to walk, Tyler's eyes swept over the room, taking in the impersonal furniture and the indifferent light. The room seemed to close in on him, a metaphor for the prison of his own making—his inability to forgive, his struggle to move on. The resentment he held for David was a constant, heavy burden that he couldn't escape, no matter how much he tried to focus on the mundane details of his office surroundings.

Tyler walked slowly to his desk, his feet dragging as if the weight of his thoughts had physical form. The cluttered surface was just as he remembered, with scattered papers, a half-empty coffee cup, and a few pens rolling around in disarray. His eyes fell on the open calendar lying in the center of the desk, a haunting reminder of the past.

The date of the trip was circled in bold red ink, standing out starkly against the white of the paper. That day had been marked as a crucial point in his career—a chance to prove himself, to climb another rung on the corporate ladder. He remembered the anticipation, the stress, the long hours of preparation leading up to it.

But now, as he stared at that circled date, all he could feel was a deep, gnawing sense of regret. The memory of that day, once filled with promise and ambition, now felt tainted, hollow. He wondered, was it really worth all of this? Was his career worth the price he'd paid?

The red circle seemed to mock him, a cruel reminder of how his priorities had led him to this point. He had sacrificed so much for that trip—time with his family, moments with his kids, the chance to be present in their lives. And for what? To end up here, in this strange, empty existence, questioning everything he had once held dear.

Tyler's fingers traced the edge of the calendar, the rough texture of the paper grounding him in the reality of his situation. The significance of that date now felt so small, so insignificant in the grand scheme of things. The trip that had once seemed like everything now felt like nothing more than a tragic mistake, a decision that had led to this unbearable loss. The question hung heavily in the air: Was it really worth it?

Just then, a solid knock echoed from the door, pulling Tyler from his thoughts. "Come in," he called out, his voice heavy with lingering sorrow. The door creaked open, and to his surprise, a young woman stepped through. She looked to be around twenty years old, her long hair cascading over her shoulders, and she was wearing a beautiful white wedding dress that seemed to glow in the dim light of the room.

Tyler blinked, taken aback by the sight. "Who are you?" he asked, his voice edged with confusion.

The woman smiled gently, her presence somehow calming. "My name is Clara," she said in a tender voice. "I like to visit everyone from time to time. It helps me feel... connected."

Tyler studied her for a moment, trying to make sense of her sudden appearance. "Why do you visit people here?" he asked, still unsure of what to make of her.

Clara's smile faltered slightly, a hint of sadness in her eyes. "I suppose I just don't like being alone. And I know how lonely it can be in these rooms. Sometimes, it helps to talk to someone who understands."

Tyler nodded slowly, still processing her words. "Do you... live here too?"

Clara nodded. "In a way, yes. We all do, in our own way." She glanced around the office, her gaze lingering on the calendar. "I see this room holds a lot of memories for you."

Tyler followed her gaze, his heart heavy as he looked at the circled date again. "Yeah," he said quietly, "it does."

Clara paused before reaching the door, turning back to Tyler with a thoughtful expression. "You know, Tyler, we have something in common," she said, her voice tinged with a mix of sorrow and acceptance.

Tyler raised an eyebrow, curious. "What do you mean?"

Clara took a deep breath, her eyes momentarily distant as if recalling a painful memory. "I died in a car accident too," she revealed, her voice steady despite the weight of the words. "I was on my way to my wedding when a drunk driver hit my car."

Tyler felt a surge of empathy, the pain of his own loss mixing with the sadness in her story. "That's... that's horrible, Clara. I'm so sorry."

Clara nodded, a faint, bittersweet smile appearing on her lips. "It was tragic, yes. But I've had a lot of time to think about it, and I've come to believe that everything happens for a reason, even when we can't understand it."

Tyler looked at her, the sincerity in her words resonate deeply within him. "You really believe that?"

Clara's eyes softened as she met his gaze. "I have to. It's the only way I've found to make peace with it all. It doesn't make the pain go away, but it helps me see the bigger picture."

Tyler remained silent for a moment, absorbing what she'd said. Her strength in accepting her fate was both comforting and inspiring, though he wasn't sure if he could ever reach that point himself.

"Maybe you're right," Tyler finally said, his voice filled with a mix of hope and doubt. "But it's hard to see the reason behind something so... senseless."

Clara nodded in understanding. "I know. It's not something you figure out overnight. But trust me, you'll get there. We all do, in our own time."

Tyler looked at Clara, curiosity getting the better of him. "Is that why you're wearing the wedding dress? Were you buried in it?"

Clara hesitated, a thoughtful expression crossing her face. "It's weird," she admitted. "I don't actually know what I was buried in. I guess it doesn't really matter here. I can change what I wear, like it's some kind of superpower. It's hard to understand, even for me."

Tyler glanced down at his own suit, the one he had been wearing on the way home that day. "I'd sure love to change out of this nightmare," he joked, though there was a hint of longing in his voice.

Clara smiles at Tyler's joke, her eyes reflecting a mixture of understanding and sorrow. "It's strange, isn't it? The way things work here. I think we all carry pieces of our old lives with us, but we're also given the ability to shape this existence in ways that might help us cope. Or at least, that's what I've figured out so far."

Tyler glances down at his suit, the weight of it suddenly feeling more symbolic than physical. "Yeah," he murmurs, "coping. Maybe that's what this all is." He looks back at Clara, curiosity piqued. "So, if you could wear anything, why the wedding dress?"

She pauses, as if searching for the right words. "Because it represents a moment in my life that was full of hope and love. Wearing it reminds me of what was important, what I was looking forward to. It helps me hold on to that, even here."

Tyler nods, a flicker of understanding passing between them. "I guess we all need something to hold on to."

Clara stood up, smoothing out the fabric of her dress. "I should be going," she said. "Thank you for letting me come visit. Maybe one day, you'll come see my room."

Tyler nodded, a faint smile on his lips. "Thanks for stopping by, Clara. And yeah, maybe I will."

Clara gave him one last warm smile before turning and heading toward the door. "Take care, Tyler," she said as she left, her voice lingering in the room like a gentle breeze.

With Clara gone, Tyler was left alone in the stark reality of his old office. The familiar surroundings, once a symbol of his achievements and aspirations, now felt like a prison. The walls seemed to close in on him, the air thick with a sense of frustration and longing.

He paced around the room, his mind racing with thoughts of his family. The calendar on his desk, still marked with the date of the fateful trip, was a cruel reminder of how his efforts to provide and support had led him to this nightmarish existence. He had always wanted to give his kids everything they needed and support his wife in every way he could. Now, those dreams felt hollow, overshadowed by the reality of his absence.

Tyler's heart ached as he thought about the time he was losing here, time that could have been spent with his family. He wished for the room to change, to escape this endless loop of regret and sorrow. All he wanted was to be with his wife and children, to hold them, to be present in their lives. The weight of his unfulfilled desires pressed heavily on him, a constant reminder of what he had lost.

Tyler took a deep breath, steadying himself against the torrent of emotions that swirled within him. He closed his eyes for a moment, trying to clear his mind. "Focus on the ultimate goal," he told himself. "Get out of this room and see your family again."

Determined, he walked over to the door, his heart pounding in his chest. He grasped the handle and tugged on it with all his strength. The door remained stubbornly closed, unmoving against his efforts. Frustration welled up inside him, but he forced himself to remain calm.

"Why am I stuck here?" he questioned aloud, his voice echoing in the confined space. He needed to understand what was keeping him in this room, to unravel the mystery of his imprisonment. His eyes scanned the office, searching for any clue or detail that might reveal why he couldn't leave.

Tyler sank into the chair behind his desk, his mind swirling with a tumult of emotions. He closed his eyes and let the quiet of the room settle around him. He needed to confront his feelings head-on, to understand what was truly keeping him trapped here.

He thought deeply about his regrets and resentments. The weight of them pressed heavily on his chest. He had always wished he had driven that night instead of David. It was a decision he now saw as a critical error, one that had led to this place. The room around him felt like a physical manifestation of his regret.

Tyler's thoughts turned to David. He had resented his co-worker for not admitting just how tired he was, for not allowing Tyler to take the wheel. It was a betrayal in his eyes, a missed chance that had dire consequences. The frustration of not having been given the opportunity to prevent the accident gnawed at him, fueling his anger and grief.

As Tyler sat there, he realized that these feelings of regret and resentment were more than just burdens; they were chains holding him to this room. He knew that to move forward, to escape this awful existence and find his family, he needed to come to terms with these emotions. Understanding and forgiveness might be the keys to unlocking the door that separated him from the life he desperately wanted to return to.

Tyler's attention snapped to the door as he heard the familiar knock. Relief washed over him at the prospect of speaking with someone who might understand his turmoil. "Come in," he called out.

Thomas appeared, his weathered face lined with empathy. He took in the office setting with a sigh, then turned his gaze to Tyler. "How are you holding up?"

Tyler's eyes were intense, filled with a mix of sorrow and resolve. "Thomas, I think I've figured out why I'm stuck in this room. It's not just about being here—it's about what's keeping me here."

Thomas nodded, his expression encouraging. "Go on."

Tyler took a deep breath, the weight of his words pressing heavily on him. "I regret not driving that night. I should have insisted on it. But more than that, I resent David for not being honest about how tired he was. I feel like if he had told me the truth, things could have been different. It's this resentment that's keeping me here, isn't it?"

Thomas listened quietly, his eyes reflecting a deep understanding. "Resentment and regret can indeed trap us in our own mindsets, just as they can trap us in physical spaces. Acknowledging them is the first step towards healing."

Tyler's voice wavered as he continued. "I keep going over what I should have done differently. I can't stop thinking about how this has cost me everything I hold dear. It feels like the walls of this room are closing in because of it."

Thomas placed a reassuring hand on Tyler's shoulder. "It's natural to have these feelings, but you need to find a way to release them. Forgiving yourself and finding peace with the past will help you move forward."

Tyler looked up at Thomas, his expression a mix of vulnerability and determination. "I want to move forward. I want to see my family again. But I don't know how to let go of this anger and regret."

Thomas gave him a sympathetic smile. "Sometimes, the hardest part is accepting that we can't change the past. But you can control how you move forward. Work through these feelings, and you'll find the path to the life you're yearning for."

Tyler nodded slowly, a flicker of hope igniting within him. "Thank you, Thomas. I'll try to work on it."

Tyler watched as Thomas prepared to leave, a thought suddenly occurring to him. "Thomas, can I ask you something?"

Thomas paused at the door and turned back, his expression open and attentive. "Of course. What's on your mind?"

Tyler took a deep breath, his curiosity outweighing his uncertainty. "I'd like to know more about you—your life. You've shared some wisdom with me, and I want to understand where you're coming from."

Thomas's eyes softened, a hint of nostalgia crossing his face. "Alright, I'll share a bit. My life was quite a journey. I'm a Civil War veteran, you see. I fought for the Union in many battles. It's a miracle, really, that I didn't die sooner."

Tyler leaned in, intrigued. "A miracle? How so?"

Thomas's gaze grew distant as he began to recount his past. "I was involved in numerous skirmishes and battles—some of which were fierce and devastating. It was only by sheer luck and a bit of providence that I survived as long as I did. Each battle, each moment, could have been my last. It's a strange feeling to reflect on all that now."

Tyler listened intently, picturing the young Thomas in the midst of the conflict. "That sounds incredibly challenging. What was it like to live through such times?"

Thomas's voice grew contemplative. "It was a time of great hardship and bravery. We fought for what we believed was right, and each day was a testament to our resolve. It wasn't easy, but it shaped me into who I am today. And in the end, it's given me a unique perspective on life, death, and what lies beyond."

Tyler nodded, absorbing the gravity of Thomas's experiences. "Thank you for sharing that with me, Thomas. It helps to understand the kind of person you were."

Thomas smiled warmly. "You're welcome. And remember, every life—whether in battle or otherwise—has its own struggles and lessons. It's important to recognize and learn from them."

Thomas stood by the door, his presence a comforting anchor in Tyler's whirlwind of emotions. He observed Tyler's intense focus on the door, sensing the determination radiating from him.

"You've got the drive to figure this out," Thomas said, his voice gentle but filled with conviction. "I can see it in you. Sometimes, finding our way out is more about facing our inner turmoil than dealing with physical barriers."

Tyler looked up, his face etched with both exhaustion and resolve. "Thank you, Thomas. I appreciate everything you've shared with me. Your support means a lot."

Thomas nodded, a smile touching his lips. "I'll leave you to your thoughts for now. Remember, you're not alone in this. You have the strength to find the answers you seek."

Tyler's eyes followed Thomas as he moved toward the door. "You're always welcome here, Thomas. Thank you for everything."

With a final nod, Thomas stepped out, closing the door behind him. Tyler was left alone once again in the dimly lit office, the weight of his emotions still heavy but tempered by the knowledge that he wasn't entirely alone in his journey.

The room remained silent except for the rhythmic ticking of a clock somewhere in the distance. Tyler took a deep breath, his gaze fixed on the door. He felt a renewed sense of purpose stirring within him—a determination to confront his regrets, to seek forgiveness, and ultimately to find a way out of this emotional prison he had created for himself.

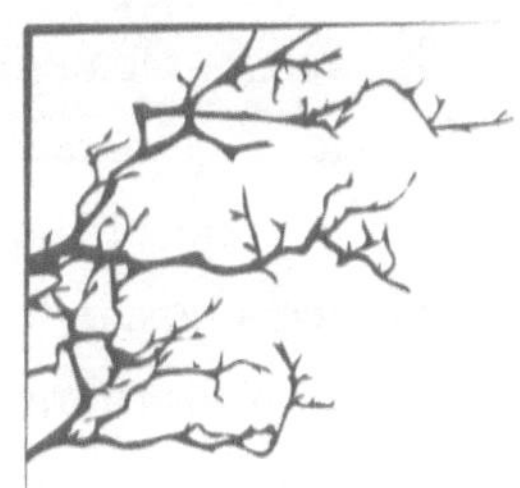

Chapter 6

The Weight of Awareness

TYLER SAT AT THE EDGE of his desk, the once-familiar office now strangely intimate. As he adjusted to the peculiarities of his new existence, he began to notice the stark differences between this state and his previous life.

He realized, with a strange mixture of relief and bewilderment, that he no longer felt physical fatigue. The heaviness of sleep that used to drag at his eyelids was gone. He didn't need rest; instead, there was a continuous awareness, a sort of heightened clarity that replaced the need for sleep.

Hunger was also a distant memory. The gnawing sensation in his stomach that had once been a constant companion was absent. He no longer needed food to sustain him, but the emotional hunger for connection and understanding seemed even more profound. It was as if the physical needs had been traded for an intensified emotional landscape.

Tyler wandered around the office, noting how his senses seemed sharper. The hum of the fluorescent lights, which he had once barely noticed, now seemed to buzz with a subtle intensity. The scent of the old leather chair, once familiar and comforting, now carried a nostalgic weight. Even the muted colors of the room, from the beige walls to the dark wood of the desk, seemed to hold a deeper significance.

His emotions were raw and vivid, amplified beyond anything he had experienced before. Memories of his family and his regrets surged through him with a clarity that was both exhilarating and overwhelming. The pain of his mistakes, the longing for his family, and the weight of his unresolved feelings with David felt more immediate and intense.

Tyler's gaze settled on the desk calendar, still open to the date of the trip. He traced the circled date with his finger, feeling the sharp pang of regret. The office was more than just a space; it was a symbol of his past decisions and the life he had been trying to build.

As he reflected on his new reality, Tyler noticed something else: the room seemed to react to his emotions. When he felt a surge of anger or sadness, the air shifted subtly, almost as if the room was mirroring his inner state.

He stood in front of the window, gazing out at a view that was both familiar and alien. The bustling cityscape outside was a reminder of the world he used to be a part of. It seemed so distant now, a world he could observe but no longer touch.

Tyler walked away from the window.

He remembered the breathing exercises his wife, Jessica, used to encourage him to practice. "They help me focus," she would say with a gentle smile, her eyes always sparkling with warmth. Tyler had often dismissed them as trivial, but now, in this strange new reality, he wondered if they might offer him some relief.

He sat cross-legged on the floor, closed his eyes and took a deep breath. He imagined Jessica's voice guiding him through the exercise, her soothing tone bringing him a semblance of calm. He inhaled deeply, feeling the imaginary air fill his lungs, and then slowly exhaled, letting go of the tension that had been building inside him. The room seemed to hold its breath along with him, and for a brief moment, the turmoil inside him quieted.

Tyler repeated the process, each breath a small escape from the weight of his emotions. The clarity he found in those moments helped him see the room not just as a prison but as a space where he might eventually find answers. The walls, though still there, felt a bit less imposing, and the flowers in the corner seemed to hold a promise of something more.

As he fell deeper into the rhythm of his breathing, he felt a subtle shift within himself—a sense of calm beginning to take root amidst the chaos of his emotions. The room around him seemed to waver, and Tyler's surroundings took on a new texture. His eyes fluttered open, and he was greeted by a profound change.

The once depressive office space was gone. In its place was the nursery from his home. The walls were painted a pastel color, and the furniture was arranged in a way that spoke of care and anticipation. A crib sat in the corner, its mobile gently spinning with painted animals. Shelves lined the walls, filled with plush toys and neatly stacked baby books. The room exudes warmth and love, a stark contrast to the starkness of the previous space.

Tyler stood up, his feet padding tenderly on the carpet. He walked over to the crib, running his fingers lightly over the thick blanket tucked inside. He felt a rush of bittersweet nostalgia wash over him. This was the room where he and Jessica had spent countless hours preparing for their children, dreaming about their future together.

His heart ached with longing as he looked around, each detail of the nursery a reminder of the life he had hoped to build. The sight of the room brought with it a flood of memories—joyful moments of anticipation, the excitement of setting up a space for new life, and the deep love he and Jessica had shared as they prepared to welcome their children into the world.

Tyler sat in the rocking chair, the gentle sway of the seat offering a fleeting sense of comfort. He closed his eyes once more, letting the memories and emotions wash over him. In this room, he felt a connection to his past and a renewed sense of purpose. Perhaps, he thought, this prison held the key to understanding his current state and finding a way forward.

He thought back to a happy moment in his life.

Jessica stood on a ladder, carefully applying a coat of pale yellow paint to the upper walls. She was humming faintly, a smile playing on her lips. Tyler was on the floor, his hands covered in blue paint as he worked on the baseboards.

"Careful up there," Tyler called with a grin. "I don't want you to fall and make me clean up a whole lot of spilled paint."

Jessica chuckled, her eyes sparkling with amusement. "Oh, don't worry. I'm not planning on falling. I'm more worried about you turning our baby's room into an abstract art piece."

Tyler chuckled, tossing a playful splash of paint onto the floor. "I think the splatter effect will add character. Besides, you're the one who wanted the room to be perfect."

Jessica glanced down, her gaze softening. "It will be perfect because we're doing it together. That's what matters. And I can't wait to see our little one's face when they're finally here."

Tyler looked up, his heart swelling with love and anticipation. "Me neither. It's going to be amazing, Jess. I'm so excited for us to be a family."

She stepped down from the ladder, wiping her hands on a rag. "Me too. You know, I love that we're doing this ourselves. It makes it feel even more special."

Tyler took her hands in his, their eyes locking in a moment of shared joy. "I wouldn't want to do it any other way. We're building something beautiful, and it's just the beginning."

As the memory faded, the room, now fully painted and decorated, stood as a testament to the love and care he and Jessica had put into it.

Tyler took a moment to let the aura of the nursery sink in. As he looked around, the initial sting of his situation began to fade, replaced by a sense of wonder. He marveled at the pastel colors and the carefully chosen decorations. There was a serene magic to the room that he hadn't noticed before.

The walls, painted in a calming shade of yellow, seemed to shimmer gently in the light. The crib, with its delicate mobile, rotated slowly, casting playful shadows on the wall. The plush toys on the shelves looked inviting, almost as if they were waiting for him to reach out and touch them.

He wandered around the room, his fingers grazing the fabric of the curtains and the texture of the carpet. The scent of fresh paint, mixed with a hint of lavender from the air freshener, filled the room, creating a soothing ambiance. He felt a gentle warmth emanating from the sunlight streaming through the window, adding to the comforting mood.

Tyler sat down in the rocking chair, letting it gently sway back and forth. He closed his eyes and listened to the creak of the chair and the distant hum of the mobile. There was a stillness here, an otherworldly tranquility that was almost enchanting. He realized that if he could set aside the reason he was here, this cage could also feel like a sanctuary—one filled with memories of love and anticipation.

It was as if the room itself was imbued with the emotions he and Jessica had invested in it. The magic wasn't just in the physical space, but in the feelings and hopes it represented. The nursery had been a canvas for their dreams, and even now, it retained a touch of that magic.

Tyler sighed deeply, allowing himself to appreciate the beauty of the room. If only he could have experienced this without the weight of his regrets and sorrow. He thought about how this place, despite being a reflection of his past, could also be a source of solace. It was a reminder of the love he had for his family and the life they had built together.

At this moment he remembered Clara saying her clothes could be changed.

Tyler closed his eyes and concentrated deeply, remembering the dark blue "#1 Dad" shirt his wife had given him. He could almost feel the familiar cotton against his skin and envision the comforting fit of his favorite blue jeans. He focused on the details: the crispness of the shirt, the worn edges of the jeans, and the warmth of the fabric.

As he let his mind clear and his focus sharpen, he felt a subtle shift within himself. The room seemed to hum with a quiet energy, and he could sense a change occurring. Slowly, he opened his eyes and looked down.

To his astonishment, Tyler saw that his outfit had transformed. Gone was the formal suit he had been wearing on the day of the accident. Instead, he was dressed in the very shirt and jeans he had envisioned. The dark blue "#1 Dad" shirt fit him perfectly, and the jeans, with their familiar comfort, felt like an embrace from the past.

He reached down and touched the fabric, marveling at how real it felt. The shirt's softness was a comforting reminder of the love Jessica had shown him, and the jeans brought a sense of familiarity that had been missing. It was as if the room had listened to his thoughts and granted him this small but significant change.

Tyler smiled, feeling a sense of relief and connection to his past life. The clothes not only represented a part of his personal history but also symbolized a bridge between his present state and the life he longed to return to. This transformation gave him a renewed sense of hope and a comforting reminder of who he was before everything changed.

With his favorite shirt and jeans on, Tyler felt a bit more like himself, and the room seemed to take on a new dimension of possibility. If he could change his appearance with his thoughts, perhaps there were other ways to influence his surroundings.

Tyler walked slowly around the room, taking in every detail as if seeing it for the first time. He ran his fingers over the edge of the bassinet, the smooth wood cool beneath his touch, evoking memories of nights spent rocking his newborns to sleep. The curtains, worn from years of sunlight, brushed against his hand as he let the fabric slip through his fingers.

Every sensation was heightened—the gentle sway of the curtains in a non-existent breeze, the faint scent of baby powder lingering in the air, the quiet creak of the floor beneath his feet. The room was alive with memories, each object a piece of the life he had cherished.

As he continued to explore, Tyler paused in the center of the room, looking around at the space that had once been filled with so much love and anticipation. It was a room that had seen the beginning of so many dreams, now repurposed into a reflection of his current reality.

He took a deep breath, the weight of the situation pressing down on him like a heavy blanket. The truth that he had been avoiding since his arrival here finally settled in. "Okay," he whispered to himself, the words feeling foreign yet inevitable. "I'm dead."

Saying it out loud, admitting it to himself for the first time, brought a strange sense of clarity. It was as if the room itself had been waiting for him to reach this conclusion, to acknowledge the truth that had been staring him in the face.

Coming to grips with this new reality, however painful, felt like a step in the right direction. Acceptance, he realized, was necessary.

Tyler decided to dedicate this time to getting used to his new existence. It was a strange, surreal experience, but one that he knew he had to embrace if he was ever going to make sense of it. He focused on the sensations around him—the feel of the bassinet's wood under his fingers, the texture of the curtains, the faint warmth that still seemed to linger in the air.

Despite the stark reality he'd acknowledged, he didn't feel dead, not in the way he'd always imagined death would be. There was no cold void, no emptiness. Instead, it was as though he had simply transitioned into a different realm, one where the rules of the physical world still applied but in a more fluid, almost graceful way.

This realm, with its shifting rooms and memories, was more than just a reflection of his past life. It was a bridge between what had been and what still could be. Tyler knew that he could feel things around him, interact with his environment, and even change aspects of it if he concentrated hard enough. This realization gave him a sense of agency, a faint glimmer of hope in a situation that had initially felt hopeless.

He wasn't sure what this realm was—somewhere between life and death, perhaps, or something else entirely—but he knew that it was his reality now. And if he could learn to navigate it, to understand its rules and limitations, maybe he could find a way to connect with the world he'd left behind, to make peace with his past and figure out what came next.

As Tyler moved around the room, absorbing the nuances of his new reality, he suddenly heard footsteps approaching the door. They were different—heavier, more deliberate, unlike the soft shuffle of the old man, the light steps of Clara, or the familiar sounds of his family's visits.

A chill ran down his spine as he froze, listening intently. The footsteps stopped just outside the door, and Tyler's heart, or whatever now passed for it, seemed to skip a beat.

"Is there someone there?" he asked, his voice tinged with curiosity and a hint of unease.

The room was silent for a moment, the air thick with anticipation. He waited, straining to hear any response, but none came. The footsteps had stopped, but the presence on the other side of the door was palpable. Tyler stood there, staring at the door, wondering who—or what—might be on the other side.

Tyler hesitated, his hand hovering just inches from the doorknob. The room was eerily quiet, the stillness amplifying the sound of his own breathing. His mind raced, torn between curiosity and fear. Just as his fingers brushed the cold metal, a sudden, loud bang echoed through the room, followed by another. Bang. Bang.

Tyler's heart pounded in his chest as he took a step back. Who could it be? Should he let them in? His thoughts tumbled over one another, each more frantic than the last. But what else could happen? He was already dead, stuck in this strange, shifting place. What more could there be?

Steeling himself, Tyler took a deep breath and, with a voice steadier than he felt, called out, "Come in."

The door swung open with a creak, and for a moment, Tyler saw nothing but darkness. Then, a figure emerged from the shadows, stepping into the light of the room. Tyler's breath caught in his throat as he recognized the man standing before him.

"Hey, buddy," the man said, his voice casual, as if they were meeting under normal circumstances.

Tyler's eyes widened in shock, his mind reeling. The room seemed to close in around him, the walls pressing closer as the weight of the moment sank in.

"David"?

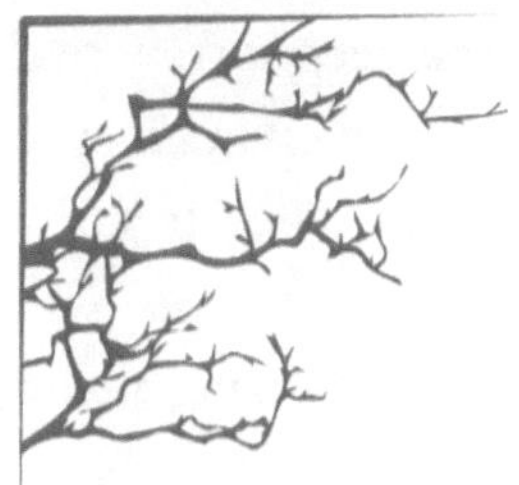

Chapter 7

A Test of Forgiveness

DAVID TOOK A STEP INTO the room, opening his mouth to speak, but Tyler's fury surged before he could get a word out.

"Don't you dare," Tyler cut him off, his voice shaking with years of bottled-up rage. "Don't you dare say anything. You took everything from me, David. Everything!"

David recoiled slightly, his face reflecting a mix of guilt and sorrow. He tried to respond, but Tyler wasn't finished.

"You were supposed to tell me if you were too tired to drive. You were supposed to let me know! But you didn't, and now I'm dead! I've lost my wife, my kids, my life—all because of you!"

Tyler's voice rose with every word, the anger pouring out like a dam finally bursting. His fists clenched at his sides as he took a step closer to David, the pain of all the missed moments—his children growing up, his wife alone—driving him forward.

"Do you know what it's like to see them and not be able to hold them? To watch them suffer and know it's all your fault because you trusted the wrong person? I was supposed to be there for them, David, and now... now I'm stuck in this place, and for what? Because you didn't think it was important to speak up?"

Tyler's voice cracked, the anger mixing with the deep sorrow that had been gnawing at him since the accident. Tears welled up in his eyes, but he refused to let them fall. He wasn't done. He needed to make David understand the gravity of what he'd done.

"You didn't just kill me, David," Tyler said, his voice lowering but no less intense. "You killed everything I was, everything I could have been. And you think you can just walk in here and... what? Apologize? Make it better? There's no fixing this!"

He stepped back, breathing heavily, his chest heaving with the effort of keeping himself from completely falling apart. All the things he'd never said, all the blame he'd kept inside, had finally erupted, and now it hung in the air between them, thick and suffocating.

Tyler stood there, his chest rising and falling rapidly as he tried to regain his breath. The room was thick with the tension of his outburst, the echoes of his words still hanging in the air. For a moment, silence reigned, the weight of Tyler's pain pressing down on both men.

David took a cautious step forward, his voice shallow and filled with regret. "Tyler... I'm sorry. I should have told you I was too tired to drive. I should have spoken up." He paused, swallowing hard as he searched for the right words. "I was exhausted, but I thought I could handle it. I didn't want to seem weak, or like I couldn't keep up. But I was wrong. I was so wrong."

He ran a hand through his hair, his eyes pleading for understanding. "I didn't realize how bad it was until it was too late. I didn't mean for any of this to happen. If I could go back... if I could change it, I would. But I can't. I can't undo what's been done."

David's voice trembled, and for the first time, Tyler saw the deep guilt etched into his face, the burden David had been carrying since the accident. "I know I took everything from you, Tyler. I know that. And I have to live with that every single day. But please... just know that I'm truly, deeply sorry. I never wanted this for you. For any of us."

He stopped, his eyes locking with Tyler's, hoping—desperately—that his words might reach him, that they might somehow begin to bridge the chasm of pain and anger that had grown between them.

Tyler stood there, the anger that had fueled his outburst slowly draining away, leaving him feeling empty and exhausted. He looked down, shaking his head slightly as he tried to process everything David had just said. The resentment that had burned so brightly moments ago began to waver, replaced by a weariness that settled deep into his bones.

When Tyler finally spoke, his voice was quieter, tinged with a sadness that hadn't been there before. "Who am I kidding?" he said, almost to himself. He raised his eyes to meet David's, the fire in them dimmed to a flicker. "I've been blaming you... but the truth is, I've been just as angry at myself. Maybe more."

Tyler paused, the weight of his own words sinking in. "I keep asking myself why I didn't take the wheel. Why didn't I see that you were too tired? I was so focused on that damn trip, on making it, that I ignored everything else. I put my career ahead of everything—my family, you, even my own instincts."

He took a deep breath, the air in the room feeling heavy. "But blaming you... blaming myself... it's not going to change anything. It's not going to bring back what I lost, what we all lost."

Tyler's voice softened, the bitterness in it replaced by a quiet resignation. "Who am I kidding, thinking that holding onto this anger would make it better? It's not helping anyone. It's just keeping me trapped here, in this... place."

David glanced around the room, his eyes landing on the familiar sight of the bassinet. A faint smile tugged at the corners of his mouth, and he shook his head slightly, a mixture of nostalgia and sadness in his expression.

"I remember coming over to help you put this bassinet together," David said, his voice tinged with a bittersweet warmth. "You were so worried it wouldn't be done by the time the baby got here."

Tyler felt a small smile break through the tension that had weighed him down. The memory of that day surfaced, vivid and clear, as if it had happened just yesterday. "Yeah," Tyler replied, the corners of his mouth lifting despite himself. "I was a nervous wreck. I wanted everything to be perfect."

David chuckled, the sound filling the room with a momentary lightness. "I think we spent more time arguing over the instructions than actually putting it together. You were convinced we were missing a piece."

Tyler let out a small laugh, shaking his head at the memory. "And it turns out I had the instructions upside down the whole time."

They both laughed, the sound echoing through the room, a brief respite from the heaviness of their situation. For a moment, it felt like they were back in the old days, just two friends sharing a laugh over something that seemed so important at the time.

But as the laughter faded, the weight of their reality settled back in, and the room grew quiet once more. Tyler looked at the bassinet, his smile fading as he was reminded of all that had been lost.

David noticed the change in Tyler's expression and sighed, his own smile fading as well. "I miss those days," he said, his voice barely above a whisper. "When things were simpler. When we thought we had all the time in the world."

Tyler nodded, the ache in his chest growing. "Yeah," he replied quietly. "So do I."

Tyler hesitated, his eyes narrowing slightly as he studied David. The question had been gnawing at him since David walked through the door. "So how did you get out of your room?" he finally asked, his voice edged with curiosity and frustration.

David sighed, rubbing the back of his neck as he struggled to find the right words. "I was trapped, Tyler. Trapped in my own guilt. Even though we both died, I couldn't leave my room. I couldn't move on because of the guilt I felt... for everything that happened."

Tyler's heart tightened at David's confession, the raw honesty hitting him harder than he expected. He remained silent, letting David continue.

"The guilt of not telling you how tired I was, the guilt of insisting on driving when I knew I shouldn't have... it weighed on me," David said, his voice almost a whisper. "And when I woke up in my own room, I couldn't move on. I was stuck, just like you."

Tyler absorbed David's words, feeling a pang of empathy despite the anger that still simmered beneath the surface. "And that's how you got out? By letting go?"

David nodded slowly. "Once I faced what happened, accepted that I couldn't change it, and forgave myself... that's when the door finally opened. It didn't make everything better, but it was a start."

Tyler looked down, the tension in his shoulders easing just a little. He sighed and then met David's gaze. "Well, I thank you for coming here," Tyler began, his voice lower, carrying a mix of regret and gratitude. "I know it must have been hard, knowing I was angry... even if that anger was as much with myself as it was with you."

David shifted slightly, a look of relief crossing his face, but he remained silent, letting Tyler say what he needed to.

"But you're my friend," Tyler continued, the words coming more freely now. "Heck, you're my kids' godfather. I should've checked on you as you drove. I should've noticed you were tired. Instead, I was selfish... focused on my own exhaustion, my own worries."

David opened his mouth to protest, but Tyler raised a hand to stop him. "No, let me finish. I was so caught up in getting home, in my own head, that I didn't think to ask if you were okay to drive. I should've been there for you, like you've always been there for me."

Tyler paused, the weight of the admission hanging in the air between them. "I'm sorry, David. I'm sorry for blaming you when I should've been looking at myself. I should've done better... as a friend, and as a father."

David's voice was steady, filled with sincerity as he responded. "You are a great father, Tyler. Don't ever doubt that."

Tyler looked up, surprised by the conviction in David's words.

"You had the holy grail," David continued. "The kids, the wife... and you earned it. The right way. You worked hard for everything you had, and you loved them more than anything. That's what really matters."

Tyler felt a lump form in his throat as David's words hit home.

"And you leave behind a great legacy," David added. "Your kids are going to grow up knowing they had the best dad in the world. That's something no accident can take away."

Tyler nodded, absorbing David's words. "Thanks, man. That means a lot."

David smiled, a hint of relief in his expression. "Anytime."

Tyler hesitated for a moment before asking, "So, are you also in this area? How does that work?"

David nodded. "Yeah, I'm close by. Just a row up from you, actually. We're neighbors in more ways than one now."

Tyler managed a small smile at that. "Good to know I'm not alone here."

David returned the smile. "You never were."

Tyler leaned in, curiosity flickering in his eyes. "So what's it like? When you leave the room, I mean. Is the world different? Dark?"

David shook his head. "It's not really any different than when we were alive. The world's still out there, just...different for us now. It does take some time to get your eyes to adjust to the light, though. You've been in here for a while, and what feels like a day in here is like a week out there."

Tyler absorbed the information, the weight of it settling in. "So, time moves faster outside?"

David nodded. "Yeah, in a way. It's weird at first, but you get used to it. The hardest part is accepting that things have changed...and learning to let go of what's keeping you in here."

Tyler's expression softened as he asked, "Do you stay out of your room a lot?"

David sighed, his gaze drifting as he thought. "I try to, but it's not easy. When I first got out, I went to check on people—family, friends. It hurt, though, seeing them live their lives, moving on. It hurt even more seeing my mom and dad, crushed over my passing. They're grieving, and it's tough to watch."

He paused, his voice lowering. "So, I decided to wait. I want to see them again, but not like this. I want to see them happy, not broken because of me. It's better that way."

Tyler nodded thoughtfully, absorbing David's words. The weight of his earlier anger seemed to lift, replaced by a wistful longing. "I understand," he said. "But have you seen my family, though? They came by to see me here in the room. But what about in the real world? Have you had any chance to check on them?"

David's expression grew reflective, his eyes drifting towards the floor as he gathered his thoughts. "Yes, I've looked in on them from afar. It's not easy, you know. I try to stay away as much as I can because seeing them in pain—it's just too hard. They're hurting, Tyler. They're carrying this weight of loss that's heavy and deep."

Tyler felt a pang of sadness, but he managed a faint smile. "I appreciate you looking in on them. How are they managing?"

David's face softened with empathy. "They're doing well considering everything. The kids—man, they've grown so much. Oliver and Grace are adjusting, and Jessica is putting on a brave face. I saw her working through the pain, trying to stay strong for them. It's hard to see them, but knowing they're managing gives me some peace."

Tyler's eyes glistened with tears, touched by the news. "It's so strange to think about how time continues on, even here. To hear that they're growing and moving forward—it's bittersweet."

David nodded, a somber smile on his face. "Time really does move differently out there. What feels like a day in here could be a week or more in the real world. I had to learn that the hard way, too. At first, I wanted to be everywhere, to see everyone, but it was too overwhelming. Now, I just try to check in when I can, but I mostly stay out of sight. It's better for them to find their own path without the constant reminder of our absence."

Tyler felt a mix of relief and sorrow. "Thank you for doing that. It's good to know that they're finding their way, even though I wish I could be there for them. I've always wanted the best for them, and hearing that they're holding up, even with the struggle, helps."

David's expression was one of understanding. "You should be proud of the legacy you left behind. Your family is strong, and they have a lot of love and support around them. They'll make it through, and they'll cherish the memories of you always."

Tyler's smile grew a little wider, though sadness lingered in his eyes. "Thank you, David. For everything. It's comforting to hear that they're okay, even if I can't be there with them."

David reached out, giving Tyler a reassuring pat on the shoulder. "Anytime, Tyler. And remember, when you're ready, you'll be able to see them again. For now, focus on finding peace with where you are. It's a journey, but it's one that can lead to understanding and acceptance."

Tyler nodded, feeling a sense of gratitude and a glimmer of hope. "I'll keep that in mind. Thanks for coming by and talking with me, David. It means more than you know."

David smiled warmly, his eyes reflecting a sense of relief. "Anytime, Tyler. I'll be around if you need me. Take care of yourself, and remember—you're not alone in this."

With that, David turned and walked towards the door. As it closed behind him, Tyler was left with a renewed sense of connection and hope. He knew the road ahead would be challenging, but with the support of friends like David, he felt a little more prepared to face it.

Tyler stood in front of the door, his heart pounding with a mix of excitement and trepidation. After David's visit, a strange feeling of resolve and readiness had washed over him. He approached the door, the sense of possibility buzzing through him like electricity.

He reached out and placed his hand on the handle. His fingers felt the cool metal, and he turned the knob slowly. The door creaked open just a crack, and Tyler could see a sliver of the world beyond, a hint of something different, something new. The gap widened slightly, and a sliver of bright light spilled into the room, creating a stark contrast with the dimly lit nursery.

Tyler hesitated. His breath caught in his throat as he stared at the opening. The world outside seemed both inviting and intimidating. It was a tangible reminder of the choices he faced—step through the door and venture into the unknown, or retreat into the familiarity of his room.

He released the handle, and the door swung back slightly before he pushed it closed again. The sudden movement was jarring, and the familiar weight of the room settled around him once more. Tyler took a deep breath, his mind racing.

Mentally ready—he could feel it. He had worked through his anger, his regrets, and his sense of loss. The conversation with David had provided clarity, and for the first time, he felt a glimmer of hope. But was he truly prepared to leave this space, to confront the reality of the world beyond the door?

Tyler paced the room, his thoughts colliding. The door was a metaphorical boundary, a line between his past and a future he couldn't fully be a part of. He wanted to see his family. Yet, uncertainty gnawed at him. What if stepping through the door brought more pain?

He thought about David's words—about seeing people in their lives, moving forward, and finding peace. Maybe he wasn't just battling his own readiness but also the implications of his presence or absence in the world.

Tyler turned back to the door, feeling its weight and presence. It was not just a physical barrier but a symbol of his internal struggle. He knew that whatever lay beyond the door could change everything.

With a sigh, Tyler placed his hand on the door again, his fingers lingering on the handle. He closed his eyes, focusing on the steady rhythm of his breath. The decision was daunting, but he had to trust that whatever choice he made would guide him towards healing.

For now, he took a step back from the door. He needed more time to understand his readiness and the consequences of his actions. As he turned away, he glanced back at the door, the light seeping through its crack a reminder of the possibilities that awaited him. He knew that the time would come when he would have to make that choice, but for now, he would continue to explore his new reality, searching for the strength and certainty to take that next step.

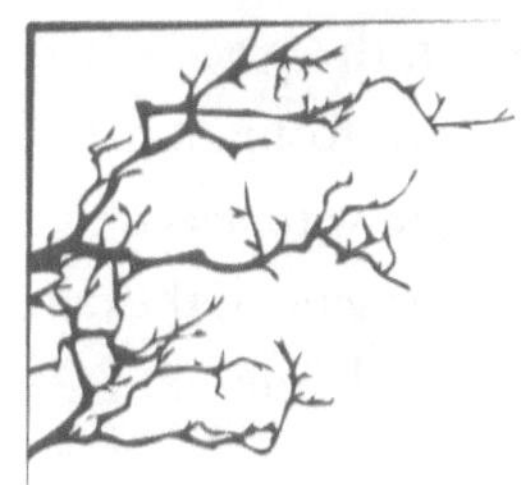

Chapter 8

Beyond The Threshold

TYLER PACED THE ROOM, his mind a storm of conflicting thoughts. He stared at the door, his heart pounding with each step. The room seemed to press in on him, the walls vibrating with the weight of his decision. The delicate hum of the nursery's lullaby, now playing on a loop, only added to his sense of urgency.

He stopped by the bassinet, running his fingers gently over the soft fabric, remembering the joy and anticipation he had felt preparing this room for his children. The sight of the nursery—once a symbol of hope and new beginnings—now felt like a painful reminder of what he had lost.

"Is it worth it?" he asked himself, the words echoing in his mind. He walked to the door, placing his hand on the handle and feeling it's cool, solid presence. The metal felt foreign in his grip, a stark contrast to the warmth and familiarity of his previous life.

He thought about his family, about Jessica and the kids. "They won't even know I'm there," he muttered, his voice barely more than a whisper. The thought of his family living their lives without him felt both comforting and heart-wrenching. What if he could see them, but they would remain unaware of his presence?

He walked over to the small desk in the corner, the place where he used to work late into the night. The room's transformation had brought back memories of deadlines and long hours, now replaced by a strange, surreal sense of time. He stared at the empty calendar, the date of the ill-fated trip circled in red, a cruel reminder of what might have been.

"What if I'm not ready?" he questioned aloud. "What if opening that door changes everything?" He could almost feel the pull of the unknown, a tangible force that tugged at his very being. The room felt like a safe cocoon, even though it was filled with reminders of his past life.

Tyler walked back to the door, his heart racing as he turned the knob. The door creaked open slightly, a sliver of light spilling into the room, illuminating the shadows. He hesitated, letting the door swing back into place, closing off the light. The decision felt immense, a choice between staying in the comfort of his past or stepping into the uncertainty of what lay beyond.

He took a deep breath, trying to calm his racing thoughts. The weight of the decision pressed heavily on him, each moment stretching into what felt like an eternity. He knew that whatever lay beyond the door was unknown, and with that knowledge came both fear and hope.

Tyler sank into the chair by the desk, his mind a whirl of emotions. "Do I stay or do I go?" he asked himself, the question echoing through his mind. His fingers drummed nervously on the armrest as he continued to weigh the pros and cons, struggling to find clarity amidst the turmoil.

Tyler's mind was a whirlwind of unresolved emotions as he sank into the meditation he had practiced before. The room, with its lingering remnants of past anxieties, seemed to close in on him. He remembered Jessica's note, a beacon of comfort amidst the storm of his thoughts: "Remember our special place."

Taking a deep breath, Tyler closed his eyes, focusing on the memory of that note. The room around him felt heavier with each breath, a sensation of both familiarity and longing. He allowed the memory of their special place to fill his mind, envisioning the hotel room from their honeymoon. The image of their shared sanctuary, a place where they had laughed, loved, and found solace, guided him through his meditation.

When he finally opened his eyes, he was enveloped by a warmth that seemed to flow through the room. The nursery had faded away, replaced by a space filled with the soothing hues of the hotel room he and Jessica had cherished. The walls were adorned with familiar decor: a delicate blend of calming blues and inviting neutrals, just as they had seen years ago.

The room was immaculate, a sanctuary of memories. The large, comfortable bed with its fluffy pillows and soft sheets was exactly as he remembered it. A small table by the window held a vase of fresh flowers, reminiscent of the ones Jessica used to pick for their room. The view outside the window was a picturesque scene of rolling hills and a serene lake, the kind of scenery that had always made them feel at peace.

Tyler walked slowly around the room, touching the furniture and feeling the textures beneath his fingers. The smooth fabric of the armchair, the cool, polished wood of the dresser—it all brought back a flood of memories. The scent of lavender, so faint but present, was a comforting reminder of the many times they had stayed here.

Sitting on the edge of the bed, Tyler let himself soak in the nostalgia. He could almost hear the echoes of their laughter, the murmur of conversations held late into the night. The room was filled with a sense of calm and joy, a stark contrast to the turmoil he had felt before.

"This is our place," he thought, a mix of relief and sadness washing over him. It was a place of peace and happiness, a haven that now existed in this new reality. The room was more than just a memory; it was a tangible piece of their shared past, a reminder of what he had lost and what he had cherished.

Tyler sat there for a while, letting himself fully embrace the serenity of the space. He closed his eyes again, focusing on the calm and happiness that the room represented. The emotional weight of his grief was still there, but it was softened by the warmth and love that this special place evoked.

In this room, amidst the echoes of their happiness, Tyler found a moment of solace. It was a reminder that even in death, some places and memories held the power to heal and comfort. And as he continued to explore this space, he felt a sense of readiness to confront whatever came next, knowing that he had a piece of his past to hold on to.

As Tyler settled into the comforting embrace of the room, he heard the familiar, gentle knock on the door. The sound was almost like a heartbeat, steady and reassuring.

"Come in," Tyler called, his voice reflecting the calm he felt in this special place.

The door creaked open, and Thomas stepped inside, his eyes widening with a mix of surprise and admiration. The room, once a symbol of Tyler's new reality, now radiated warmth and tranquility. Thomas took in the scene with a genuine smile.

"Beautiful room," Thomas said, his voice filled with genuine appreciation. "It seems like you've found a sanctuary of your own."

Tyler looked around, noticing how the room seemed to invite a sense of peace and happiness. The familiar surroundings of their honeymoon retreat felt like a gentle embrace, a sanctuary carved from memory and love.

"It is," Tyler agreed, feeling the sincerity in Thomas's words. "It's where Jessica and I spent some of our happiest moments. It feels like home, even now."

Thomas nodded, his gaze lingering on the soft hues and carefully arranged furnishings. "I see that. It's amazing how our memories can shape the places we find comfort in. It's a beautiful reflection of what mattered most to you."

Tyler felt a sense of validation. Thomas's recognition of the room's significance reinforced the importance of holding on to these precious memories. The room was more than just a space; it was a testament to the life he had lived and the love he had shared.

Thomas took a moment to absorb the room's tone, then turned back to Tyler with a thoughtful expression. "I can see you're finding your way here. Sometimes, finding comfort in our memories is the first step toward healing."

Tyler nodded, feeling a renewed sense of hope. "It's a start. It's helping me come to terms with everything."

Thomas's smile was both understanding and encouraging. "You're doing well. Remember, it's not just about moving forward; it's about finding peace with where you've been. This room, your memories—they're part of that journey."

Tyler took a deep breath, the weight of his thoughts pressing heavily on him. He approached Thomas, who was still taking in the serene beauty of the room.

"Thomas, I could use your advice," Tyler said, his voice steady but tinged with uncertainty. "David came by earlier, and we had a positive conversation. It made me think that maybe I'm ready to open the door, but I'm scared. How do I know if it's the right time?"

Thomas turned to face Tyler, his expression thoughtful. He could see the conflict etched in Tyler's eyes, the struggle between the desire to move forward and the fear of the unknown.

"Of course, Tyler," Thomas replied with a reassuring nod. "Opening the door is a significant step. It's understandable to feel apprehensive. Here's what I can tell you: you've made a lot of progress. Facing your fears, confronting your regrets, and finding a sense of peace in this room are all steps in the right direction."

Tyler listened intently, hoping for guidance that would help him make sense of his emotions.

"When you're ready to open the door," Thomas continued, "it's important to remember that it's not just about what you're leaving behind but also about what you're moving toward. The door represents a new beginning, but it's also a chance to find closure and acceptance."

Tyler nodded, absorbing Thomas's words. "But how do I know if I'm truly ready? What if I open it and it's not what I expect?"

Thomas placed a comforting hand on Tyler's shoulder. "Sometimes, the only way to find out is to take the step. You've faced your fears and made peace with your past. The fear you're feeling is natural, but it's also a sign that you're on the brink of something new. Trust yourself and the progress you've made."

Tyler's mind raced as he considered Thomas's advice. He had confronted his resentment, found solace in his memories, and shared a meaningful conversation with David. The idea of opening the door seemed less daunting with Thomas's words in mind.

Thomas smiled, his eyes filled with encouragement. "You have the strength to face whatever comes next. If you're feeling ready, then take that step. And remember, it's okay to feel scared. It's part of the journey."

Tyler took another deep breath, feeling a sense of resolve beginning to build within him. He knew the decision to open the door was his alone, but with Thomas's advice, he felt more confident in his ability to face whatever lay beyond.

"Thank you, Thomas," Tyler said sincerely. "I appreciate your guidance."

Thomas gave Tyler a reassuring smile, his presence a comforting anchor in the midst of Tyler's inner turmoil.

"Anytime, Tyler," Thomas said, his tone gentle yet firm. "Take your time to think about your decision. Remember, this is your journey, and you have the strength to navigate it."

Tyler nodded, feeling a sense of gratitude for Thomas's support. The weight of the decision still loomed large, but Thomas's words had provided him with a measure of clarity.

Thomas turned to leave, his movements deliberate and calm. As he reached the door, he paused and looked back at Tyler. "If you do decide to open the door and step out, come find me. I'll be here to support you, no matter what."

Tyler watched as Thomas exited the room, leaving him alone with his thoughts. The serene hotel room around him felt like a cocoon, a place where he could reflect and make his choice with the time and space he needed.

As the door clicked shut behind Thomas, Tyler took a deep breath and turned his attention to the door that had been both a barrier and a promise. He knew that the decision to open it was his alone to make, but with Thomas's encouragement, he felt a renewed sense of hope and resolve.

Tyler approached the door with a sense of determination. His heart pounded in his chest, each step filled with a mix of fear and resolve. He reached out and grasped the handle, its cool metal sending a shiver through his fingers. With a deep breath, he turned the knob and pulled the door open.

As the door swung wide, a bright, blinding light poured through, engulfing him in a warm, radiant glow. The intensity of the light made him squint, but he felt a sense of liberation and anticipation. He took one last look at the room he was leaving behind, the cozy hotel space that had become his sanctuary.

With a final, steadying breath, Tyler stepped through the doorway. The light enveloped him completely, and for a moment, he felt suspended in a surreal, almost otherworldly space. The sensation was both exhilarating and overwhelming.

As Tyler's eyes adjusted to the fading light, the world around him slowly came into focus. He found himself standing in a sprawling cemetery, where the headstones rose like monumental pillars, their grandeur exaggerated in the afterlife. Each stone was adorned with a door handle, giving the impression that each resting place was a portal to another realm.

He turned to examine his own headstone, noticing its imposing size. The inscription read, "Tyler Lawson, a loving father and husband." The familiar words, carved in elegant script on the door of his stone, filled him with a profound sense of warmth and peace. The phrase resonated deeply within him, a testament to the love and life he had lived.

A smile gently spread across his face as he took in the sight. The cemetery, though somber, held an unexpected beauty. The light seemed softer here, the character serene. Tyler felt a mixture of relief and contentment, knowing that this was a reflection of his life and the love he had cherished.

He glanced around, seeing other doors with inscriptions that told stories of lives lived and loved. The cemetery felt like a sacred space, each stone a monument to the people who had once walked the earth. Tyler's heart swelled with a sense of belonging, as if he had finally found his place in this new realm.

With renewed hope, Tyler took a deep breath, feeling the weight of his past regrets lift slightly. He was ready to explore this new world, to find his way forward, and perhaps, to continue his journey of understanding and healing in the afterlife.

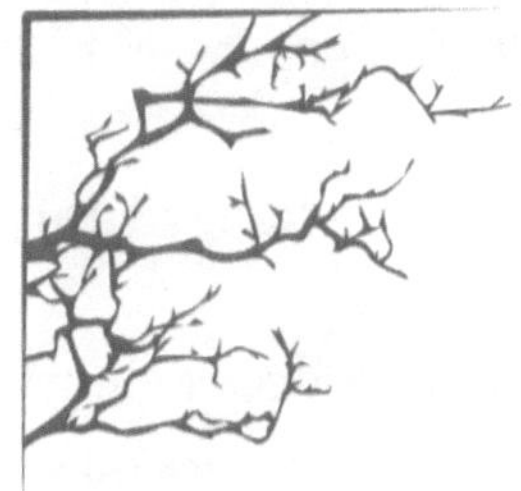

Chapter 9

The Road Back

THE LIGHT WAS BRIGHT and ethereal, bathing everything in an otherworldly glow. As he walked, the ground beneath him felt solid, yet his steps were silent.

He wandered through the rows, his eyes scanning the names etched into the stones. Each door was unique, reflecting something personal about the person it marked.

Finally, Tyler came upon a grave marked with a familiar name: David Turner. The stone was unassuming, but the door on it held the same kind of significance as his own.

Tyler approached the grave with a sense of purpose, his heart pounding with anticipation. He had seen the door on David's headstone, just like his own. With a deep breath, he knocked gently on the door.

"Come in," came David's voice from inside.

Tyler pushed open the door, revealing a warm, rustic interior. The room inside looked like a cozy cabin, with wooden walls, a stone fireplace, and a large, comfortable armchair positioned by a window that framed a picturesque forest view. The scent of pine and earth filled the air.

David, sitting comfortably in the armchair, looked up with a welcoming smile. "Hey, Tyler. It's good to see you."

Tyler stepped inside and took in the tranquil surroundings. "This room is amazing. I didn't expect you'd have a cabin."

David chuckled. "Yeah, it's my father's old hunting lodge. It always brought me peace. I guess it's kind of like my own little sanctuary now."

Tyler nodded, appreciating the serene ether. "It looks like a perfect spot for reflection. A special place just for you. Thanks for sharing it with me."

David smiled and gestured to the armchair. "Make yourself at home. It's nice to have a friend visit."

Tyler stepped into the room, and David's warm, inviting space came into view. The room was cozy, resembling a rustic cabin, with wooden walls and a crackling fireplace that gave off a gentle, flickering light. A large, leather rocking chair sat in the center, and Tyler made his way to it, sinking into its familiar creak with a sigh of relief.

"Thank you for letting me in," Tyler said, looking around with appreciation. He paused, gathering his thoughts. "I'm going to see my family now. Is there anything I should know before I go?"

David nodded, his face reflecting a mix of understanding and encouragement. "Yes, there are a few things you should be aware of," he began. "Now that you're no longer living, you can move through the world a bit more quickly. You might find it easier to get to places that used to be far away. Some who have been here for a long time have even discovered ways to move around almost instantaneously, though I haven't quite figured out how to do that myself yet."

Tyler's eyes widened with the possibilities. "So, I can travel faster? That's good to know."

David smiled. "Exactly. It's one of the few perks of being in this realm. Just keep in mind that your emotions and focus play a big part in how smoothly things go. When you're ready, you'll find that things fall into place."

Tyler nodded, feeling a renewed sense of determination. "Thank you, David. I'll remember that."

David gave a reassuring nod. "Go on, then. Your family is waiting. And remember, if you need anything, you know where to find me."

With that, Tyler stood, offering David a grateful smile before turning to leave. As he walked back towards the door, he felt a mix of excitement and apprehension about the journey ahead.

Tyler approached the edge of the cemetery, feeling a surge of anticipation as he took his first step beyond the wrought iron gates. The moment his foot touched the pavement, he sensed a remarkable change. Each step he took felt effortless, as if he were gliding across the ground. The distance between his current position and his destination seemed to shrink with every stride.

He marveled at the sensation, realizing David's words were true. The world around him seemed to blur slightly, and he could cover ground much faster than he had ever thought possible. A sense of exhilaration mixed with a profound sense of freedom filled him. The concrete beneath his feet felt different—almost like a trampoline propelling him forward.

With a smile on his face, Tyler headed north, the direction that would lead him to his home. The familiar sights of the street began to emerge as he moved swiftly past them, his heart pounding with a blend of excitement and nervousness. He could hardly believe how quickly the landscape was changing before his eyes. Every block seemed to pass in the blink of an eye, and he felt a renewed sense of hope and determination.

The journey that had once felt like an insurmountable distance now seemed like a mere stroll. Tyler's thoughts were solely focused on reuniting with his family. He embraced the new speed, using it to fuel his anticipation as he made his way towards the place he longed to be—the place where his heart had always belonged.

Tyler arrived at his home in what felt like an instant. The white house with its light blue shutters stood just as he remembered it, nestled behind a neat, fenced-in backyard. The familiar sight of the house filled him with a deep, comforting sense of nostalgia.

He paused at the edge of the property, taking a moment to fully absorb the scene before him. The faint hum of the television drifted through the open windows, carrying the sounds of his son's favorite kids' show. The laughter and playful chatter from the screen seemed to weave through the air, mingling with the sounds of the evening.

Tyler's heart swelled as he gazed at the house. It was a beacon of warmth and happiness—a symbol of everything he had worked for and cherished. The vibrant colors of the house, the green of the lawn, and the gentle sway of the trees in the breeze all seemed to come alive in this moment of clarity.

He stood there, savoring the peacefulness and the familiar surroundings. For a brief moment, he felt as though he were still part of the world he had left behind. The house, the yard, and the sounds from inside were all reminders of the life he had loved so deeply.

Taking a deep breath, Tyler felt a mixture of excitement and apprehension. He was about to see his family again, but the experience would be different from what he had known.

Tyler approached the front door with a mixture of anticipation and nerves. He reached out, his hand poised to grasp the door knob, but his fingers passed right through it as if it were nothing more than a mirage.

He paused for a moment, a wry smile tugging at his lips. "Of course," he muttered to himself. It was a surreal realization that the physical barriers of his old life no longer applied to him.

With a deep breath, Tyler stepped forward and walked straight through the door. The sensation was disconcertingly smooth, as if the door wasn't even there. There was no resistance, no change in temperature—just the seamless transition from one side to the other.

Inside, the house was just as he remembered, but it felt strangely delicate. The air was filled with the comforting sounds of his son's show, and the warm glow of the lights cast familiar patterns on the walls. Tyler took a moment to absorb it all, letting the sense of home wash over him.

He moved further into the house, every step bringing him closer to his family. The familiar scents, the cozy furniture, and the cozy decor all surrounded him, reinforcing the bittersweet reality of his new existence.

Tyler moved quietly through the living room, his heart pounding with a mix of excitement and anxiety. The constant hum of the television faded as he approached the kitchen. The familiar sound of his wife's voice, warm and loving, called out, "Oliver, Grace, dinner time!"

The sound of dishes clinking and the scent of cooking food drifted through the air, filling him with a poignant sense of nostalgia. Tyler felt a lump in his throat as he imagined his family gathered around the table, just as they had countless times before.

He continued toward the kitchen, each step a blend of hope and trepidation. As he neared the doorway, he could see the glow of the kitchen lights casting a comforting warmth on the floor. The sound of his children's laughter, the rhythmic clatter of utensils, and his wife's gentle hum as she prepared dinner created a symphony of home that made his heart ache with longing.

Tyler paused at the kitchen entrance, taking a deep breath to steady himself. The scene before him was both heartwarming and heart-wrenching—a vivid reminder of what he had lost and what he still held dear.

Tyler took a deep breath and walked into the kitchen, his heart racing. The kitchen was alive with the warmth of home—the table set for dinner, with Jessica bustling around, placing dishes on the table. Oliver and Grace were already seated, their faces lit up with excitement.

Jessica turned to her children, her voice gentle and curious. "So, how was school today? Did anything interesting happen?"

Oliver grinned, his eyes twinkling with mischief. "You wouldn't believe it, Mom! Mrs. Carter asked us to write about our favorite animals, and I wrote about a dragon. I said dragons were my favorite because they could breathe fire and fly, and Jake said he doesn't believe in dragons. I told him he's missing out!"

Grace giggled, her small hands clasped around her fork. "I bet Jake was jealous he didn't get a dragon for his favorite animal!"

Jessica laughed, shaking her head as she sat down at the table. "You always have the best stories, Oliver. And Grace, how was your day?"

Grace looked up, her cheeks flushed with enthusiasm. "We did a craft today! I made a rainbow with all the colors I could find. Mrs. Lee said it was the most colorful rainbow she'd ever seen."

Jessica's smile widened as she served the food. "That sounds wonderful, sweetie. I can't wait to see it."

Tyler stood silently at the edge of the room, his heart swelling with emotion. The sight of his family, their voices blending with the everyday sounds of their life, was both a balm and a bittersweet reminder of everything he missed.

Jessica glanced around the table, her eyes warm and full of love. "I'm so proud of you both. You're doing great in school and you make everyday brighter. Now, let's enjoy dinner. Oliver, tell us more about your dragon story."

As Tyler watched, he saw Jessica's face light up with affection for her children, her love evident in every word and gesture. He could see the little moments that made their family special, and he felt a profound sense of both joy and sorrow.

As Tyler stood in the kitchen, taking in the heartwarming scene of his family, the familiar sound of claws clicking on the tile floor caught his attention. Scout, the family dog, trotted in from the living room, his tail wagging energetically. His ears perked up, and his nose twitched as he looked directly at Tyler.

Scout's eyes seemed to lock onto Tyler's presence, and with an excited bark, he bounded towards him. His joyous barks filled the room, causing Jessica to look up from the table with a mixture of confusion and concern.

"Scout, what's got into you?" Jessica said, her voice carrying a hint of amusement as she tried to calm the excitable dog. But Scout wouldn't be pacified. He continued barking and wagging his tail, clearly eager to get closer to Tyler.

Jessica sighed, shaking her head with a smile. "Alright, Scout. Come here, boy."

She led Scout to the door, coaxing him with gentle words. "Come on, Scout. Let's get you outside for a bit."

As Scout approached the door, his eyes remained fixed on Tyler. He seemed to sense something, or someone, beyond the physical barrier. With a final, hopeful bark, he followed Jessica out into the backyard.

Tyler watched as the door swung open and Jessica led Scout outside. The dog's barks faded into the distance, but Tyler could still feel the warmth of Scout's enthusiastic welcome. The brief interaction left him with a strange mix of comfort and melancholy. It was as if Scout's reaction was a reminder of the bond that still connected him to his family, even though he could only watch from afar.

As Jessica gently closed the door behind her, Tyler's heart ached with longing. He took a deep breath, summoning every ounce of emotion he had left. With a whisper, barely more than a breath, he said, "I love you."

Jessica froze. For a moment, it seemed as if time itself had stopped. Her eyes darted around the room, searching, as if she felt a presence she couldn't quite place. She turned in Tyler's direction, her face pale and her eyes glistening with unshed tears. "I miss you, Tyler," she whispered, her voice breaking with emotion.

The room seemed to hold its breath. Jessica's expression wavered between vulnerability and strength. She took a moment to compose herself, her shoulders rising and falling as she fought to maintain her composure. With a final, deep breath, she gathered herself and returned to the kitchen table, her face now a mask of courage for the sake of their children.

Sitting down, she picked up her fork and resumed the conversation, her voice steady despite the turmoil she felt inside. Tyler watched, his heart heavy with the bittersweet realization that while he could reach out in spirit, the tangible connection with his family was something he could only experience through their reactions and emotions.

Tyler stood in the corner of the kitchen, watching as Jessica gently ushered Oliver and Grace towards their bedtime routine. The familiarity of the scene tugged at his heart. He could hear Jessica's voice as she guided them upstairs, the echoes of their playful banter filling the house.

Once they reached the top of the stairs, Jessica turned on the nightlight in Grace's room, casting a warm glow across the pink walls. Tyler followed quietly, feeling an overwhelming sense of love and loss. Jessica helped Grace into her bed, tucking the covers around her snugly, then did the same for Oliver.

"Alright, little ones, settle down," Jessica said with a tender smile. "It's story time."

Both kids perked up, their eyes wide with anticipation. Tyler watched as Jessica pulled up a small chair next to Grace's bed, where Oliver had already plopped down with a pillow, ready to listen.

"Tonight's story," Jessica began, her voice taking on a magical tone, "is about a brave little fox named Felix."

Grace and Oliver exchanged excited glances.

"Felix lived in a big, dark forest," Jessica continued, "but he wasn't afraid. You see, Felix had a special gift. He could run faster than any other animal in the forest, so fast that he could outrun his own shadow."

Tyler watched, entranced, as Jessica spun the tale. He could almost feel the warmth of those nights when he used to tell stories to the kids.

"One day," Jessica said, "Felix found out that a big storm was coming. The wind howled through the trees, and the animals were scared. But Felix knew he had to do something. So, he ran faster than ever before, gathering all the animals and leading them to a safe, hidden cave deep in the forest."

Grace's eyes were wide with wonder, and Oliver leaned forward, hanging on every word.

"But just as they reached the cave, the storm arrived. Thunder roared, and lightning flashed, but Felix didn't stop. He stood at the cave's entrance, making sure all the animals were safe inside. He was brave, even when the storm seemed to be at its worst."

Tyler could see the pride in Jessica's eyes as she looked at her children, her voice steady and comforting.

"And when the storm finally passed," she said in a warming voice, "the sun came out, and a beautiful rainbow appeared across the sky. Felix knew that he had done something very special, something brave and kind. The animals of the forest never forgot his courage, and they always remembered him as the little fox who could outrun his own shadow."

There was a moment of silence as Jessica finished the story. Grace and Oliver were already drifting off, their eyelids heavy with sleep. Jessica leaned down to kiss them each on the forehead, whispering goodnight.

Tyler felt a deep ache in his chest, watching the intimate moment. He wanted nothing more than to be there, to be the one tucking them in and telling them stories.

Jessica turned off the light, leaving only the glow of the nightlight. She quietly left the room, closing the door behind her. Tyler stayed for a moment longer, his eyes lingering on his children as they slept peacefully, before following her out of the room.

Tyler quietly followed Jessica into the living room, his heart heavy with the weight of what he had just witnessed. He watched as she sank into the couch, her shoulders slumping in exhaustion. The room was dimly lit, the only light coming from a small lamp in the corner, casting shadows across the room.

Jessica sat in silence for a few moments, her hands resting in her lap, her eyes distant. Then, as if needing to release the thoughts that had been swirling in her mind, she began to speak, her voice soft and filled with emotion.

"I miss you," she whispered, her voice trembling slightly. "The kids miss you. I'm trying my best, I promise I am. But it's so hard, Tyler. It's so hard without you."

Tyler's heart ached as he listened. He wanted nothing more than to reach out, to comfort her, to tell her that she wasn't alone. But all he could do was stand there, helpless, watching the love of his life pour her heart out into the empty room.

Jessica continued, her voice cracking as she spoke. "I never realized how much I relied on you until you were gone. I feel like I'm failing, like I'm not enough for them. But I have to keep going. I have to be strong for them. For you."

Tyler took a deep breath, his emotions overwhelming him. "You are my everything," he said, hoping somehow she could hear him. "More than you know. More than you ever knew. And I'm sorry... I'm sorry it took this happening for me to see just how amazing you are. I took you for granted, Jess. I never told you enough how much you mean to me."

Jessica's eyes welled up with tears as she leaned back against the couch, staring up at the ceiling. "I just wish I could hear your voice again," she whispered. "To know that you're okay, wherever you are. I wish I could feel you here with me."

Tyler felt a lump in his throat, his own eyes stinging with unshed tears. He wished he could find a way to let her know he was there, that he was watching over her and the kids. But all he could do was stand by, a silent witness to her grief and his own regret.

"I'm here," he said delicately, his voice full of longing. "I'm right here, Jess. And I'm so sorry I didn't appreciate you the way I should have. You were always enough, more than enough. I see that now, and I wish I could tell you."

Jessica wiped away a tear that had escaped down her cheek, her expression softening as she continued to stare at the ceiling. "I love you, Tyler," she whispered. "I'll always love you. No matter what."

"I love you too," Tyler replied, his voice breaking. "More than anything in this world."

For a moment, the room was filled with a profound silence, as if the very air was holding its breath. Tyler could almost feel a connection, a thread of understanding passing between them. It was as though, despite the distance between life and death, their hearts were still linked, still speaking the words that needed to be said.

Jessica finally stood up, taking a deep breath to steady herself. She wiped her eyes, squared her shoulders, and walked toward the hallway. Before she disappeared into the darkness, she paused, as if sensing something. She turned slightly, looking over her shoulder with a sad, wistful smile.

"Goodnight, Tyler," she whispered, almost as if she knew he was there.

Tyler stood rooted to the spot, his heart aching with love and regret. "Goodnight, Jess," he whispered back. "I'll always be with you."

And with that, Jessica turned and walked down the hallway, leaving Tyler alone in the dimly lit living room, surrounded by memories and an unspoken promise that, no matter what, he would always be by her side.

Tyler stepped out of the house, the familiar warmth of his home fading as he crossed the threshold and returned to the quiet, still world of the cemetery. The night air was cool and crisp, a stark contrast to the warmth inside. As he walked down the empty streets, his mind replayed the scenes he had just witnessed—Jessica's strength, the kids' laughter, and the poignant moments that had unfolded before him.

His steps were slower now, more measured, as if the weight of everything he had seen and felt was pressing down on him. The journey back to the cemetery, which had felt so swift on his way there, now seemed to stretch out, giving him time to process the emotions swirling inside him.

When he finally reached the cemetery, the sight of the headstones, all lined up in their silent rows, brought a strange sense of peace. The silent land, once so foreign and eerie, now felt almost familiar—a resting ground not just for bodies, but for thoughts, memories, and the emotions that had nowhere else to go.

Tyler found himself standing outside his room, staring at the door with his name etched into it. The words "Tyler Lawson, a loving father and husband" were inscribed with a care that somehow managed to encapsulate both pride and sorrow. He traced the letters with his eyes, the phrase resonating deeply within him. It was a reminder of who he had been, what he had accomplished, and the legacy he had left behind.

But it was also a reminder of what he had lost.

He stood there, hands in his pockets, feeling the cool stone beneath his feet. The silence of the cemetery was comforting, yet it amplified the thoughts racing through his mind. Everything he had just seen—the joy and the pain—lingered with him. Jessica's resilience, the children's innocence, and the love that still bound them all together even in his absence. It was a lot to take in, and he couldn't help but feel a mix of emotions—pride, regret, love, and a deep, aching longing.

"Was I really ready to leave them?" he thought, staring at the door as if it could give him the answers he sought. "Did I do enough? Did they know how much I loved them?"

The questions were endless, swirling around in his mind like autumn leaves caught in a gust of wind. He thought back to the moments he had taken for granted, the times he had let work or exhaustion come between him and his family. The regret was sharp, but so was the realization of just how much they had meant to him—how much they still meant to him.

Tyler sighed, his breath misting in the cool night air. The truth was, nothing could change what had happened. But standing here now, outside the door to his resting place, he realized something important. His life had ended, but his love for his family had not. That love was what gave him the strength to see them again, to cherish those moments, even if they were painful.

He took a deep breath, letting the crisp air fill his lungs. He knew he couldn't stay out here forever, lost in thought. There were things he still needed to do, decisions he needed to make.

But for now, he allowed himself this moment—this quiet reflection outside the door that marked his place in the world, both in life and in death. The cemetery, with its silent, watchful stones, seemed to understand. It offered no judgment, only the quiet companionship of those who had passed on before him.

Tyler stands outside his room, lost in thought, when Clara and Thomas approach. Clara is the first to speak, "We knew you went to see them. How are you holding up?"

Tyler takes a deep breath, his emotions still swirling from the visit. "I saw them... Jess, the kids. It was harder than I imagined, but at the same time, it was comforting. I watched Jess put the kids to bed, and I realized just how much I took for granted. I always thought I had time... but seeing them like that, knowing I can't be with them, it hurts."

Thomas nods, a look of understanding in his eyes. "It's natural to feel that way, Tyler. But you went and saw them, and that's a step forward."

Clara steps closer, offering a gentle smile. "You're stronger than you think. And you're not alone in this. We're here for you."

Tyler looks at them both, grateful for their presence. "Thank you. It means a lot to have you two around."

Thomas claps a hand on Tyler's shoulder. "Remember, it's not about what you can't do, but what you choose to do with the time you have left—here or otherwise."

Tyler offers a small smile of gratitude to Clara and Thomas. "Thanks for everything. I just need some time to myself."

Clara nods understandingly, while Thomas gives him a reassuring pat on the back. "Take all the time you need, Tyler. We're just a knock away."

With a final glance at them, Tyler turns and walks back to his room. As he opens the door and steps inside, he's taken aback by what he sees. The room has changed again. Instead of the familiar settings he's grown accustomed to, it's now the living room from his home—the very place where he last saw Jessica.

The details are perfect, right down to the couch where she had sat, speaking her heart out as if she knew he was there. The glow of the lamp, the warmth of the room, the faint scent of her perfume still lingering in the air—it's all here, just as it was in that moment.

Tyler stands in the doorway, his breath catching as he takes it all in. The room is alive with memories, filled with the echoes of their life together. It's almost too much, too real, as if he could reach out and touch the life he's left behind.

He walks slowly over to the couch and sits down, his hand brushing against the fabric where Jessica had been. A wave of emotions crashes over him—love, regret, longing. He closes his eyes, imagining her there with him, her presence so tangible it's as if she's right beside him.

"Jessica," he whispers, his voice thick with emotion. "I wish I was there with you."

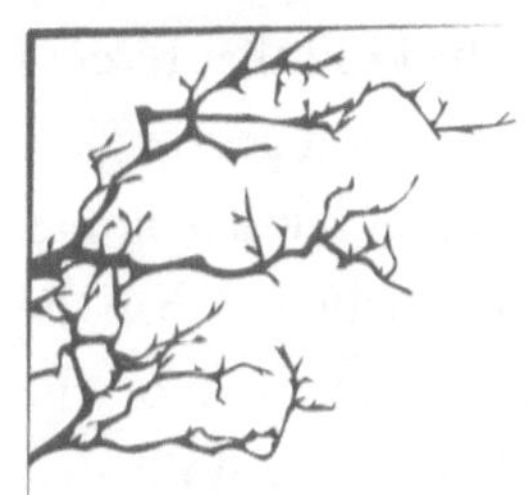

Chapter 10

A Glimpse of What Could Have Been

THIS ROOM, WHERE HE last felt close to her, now serves as a bittersweet sanctuary. It's a connection to the world he can no longer be a part of, a reminder of everything he's lost and everything he still holds dear.

Tyler sat quietly in the living room, his favorite armchair cradling him in its familiar embrace. Days had drifted by since he last stepped outside, but it didn't bother him. The usual restlessness that had accompanied him was gone, replaced by a sense of peace that had settled deep within his chest.

The air around him was warm, like a blanket on a cool autumn evening, carrying with it the faint scent of lavender from the candle Jessica used to burn in this very room. He could almost hear her humming in the kitchen, the clinking of dishes as she put them away, the sound blending with the distant laughter of their children from days long past. His ears strained to catch these echoes, knowing they weren't real, but cherishing them all the same.

The room itself was bathed in a golden light, the kind that filtered through the sheer curtains in the late afternoon. It cast a gentle glow on the hardwood floor, warming the space in a way that felt like home. The colors of the room were vivid, almost more vibrant than he remembered—Jessica's favorite throw draped over the back of the couch, the deep blue of the cushions, the pale yellow of the walls that always seemed to make the room feel brighter, even on cloudy days.

His fingers brushed against the fabric of the armchair, the worn leather smooth under his touch, comforting in its familiarity. The texture brought back memories of countless evenings spent right here, talking, laughing, and simply being together. He could almost taste the bitterness of the coffee they used to share, the way it lingered on his tongue long after the cup was empty, mixed with the sweetness of Jessica's homemade cookies.

There was no sadness in him now. Instead, he felt fulfilled, like a man who had finally found the answer to a question that had haunted him for too long. Knowing his family was okay, that they were carrying on even in his absence, had given him a peace he hadn't known he needed. The weight of the uncertainty that had once pressed down on him was gone, replaced by a quiet contentment.

Tyler closed his eyes, letting the sounds, scents, and sensations of the room wash over him. He wasn't avoiding the world outside; he was simply savoring this moment, knowing it was a gift. This room, this space, had become a sanctuary—a place where he could hold onto the best parts of his life, without the sorrow that had once tainted his memories. And for now, that was enough.

Tyler was lost in the warmth of his memories when a soft knock on the door pulled him back to the present. He opened his eyes, the golden light of the room still wrapping him in it's comforting embrace. For a moment, he hesitated, then called out, "Come in."

The door creaked open, and David stepped inside, his presence bringing a slight shift to the room's climate. David's face was a mix of concern and relief as he looked at Tyler.

"Hey, Tyler," David greeted, a small smile playing on his lips. "I wanted to check on you. It's been a few days since you left your room. I was getting a little worried."

Tyler nodded, motioning for David to take a seat. "I've been here," he said, his voice calm and steady. "Just...taking it all in."

David sat down across from Tyler, his eyes scanning the room. "I can see why. This place... it feels like home, doesn't it?"

Tyler smiled, glancing around at the familiar surroundings. "It does. It really does. I've been thinking a lot, David. About everything—about my family, about what's next."

David leaned forward, his expression serious now. "I get that. It's a lot to process. But I wanted to make sure you're okay. I know how easy it is to get lost in here, especially when everything feels so... perfect."

Tyler appreciated David's concern, sensing the genuine care behind his words. "I'm okay. I think I needed this time, you know? To find some peace."

David shifted in his seat, looking uncharacteristically nervous. He rubbed the back of his neck, a familiar gesture Tyler recognized from their time together in the living world. It was the way David always acted when he was unsure about something.

"There's something I need to ask you, Tyler," David began, his voice tinged with hesitation. Tyler leaned in slightly to show he was listening.

"Of course, David. What's on your mind?" Tyler asked.

David took a deep breath, his eyes dropping to the floor as if searching for the right words. "There's this girl...I liked her for a long time. I never really got the chance to ask her out, though. I planned to do it when we got back from that trip, but...well, you know how that turned out." He gave a small, humorless chuckle, but there was an unmistakable sadness in his eyes.

Tyler watched him carefully, sensing the weight of what David was about to say next.

"She didn't even know how I felt," David continued, his voice quieter now. "But the feelings are still there, Tyler. I don't know if it's stupid to think like this, but...I just need to know she's okay. Maybe it's selfish, I don't know, but I can't stop thinking about her."

David looked up, meeting Tyler's gaze with an expression that was both hopeful and vulnerable. "I was wondering if you'd go with me to check on her. I'm not even sure if I should, but... I just need to see her, even if she never knew how I felt."

Tyler nodded slowly, understanding the mix of emotions David was grappling with. "You've been carrying this with you all this time," he said gently. "It's not stupid, David. It's human. Wanting to know she's okay, that's something anyone would feel."

David let out a breath he hadn't realized he was holding. "So, will you come with me? I'm not sure I can do it alone."

Tyler placed a reassuring hand on David's shoulder. "Of course, I will. We'll go together. Sometimes, we just need to see things through, even if it's just for our own peace of mind."

David nodded, his face softening with gratitude. "Thanks, Tyler. I don't know what I'd do without you, man."

Tyler smiled, a warmth in his chest that hadn't been there before. "We'll figure it out together, David. Let's go see what's out there."

Tyler followed David out of the room, the cool air of the cemetery brushing against his skin as they stepped outside. The silence between them was comfortable, filled with unspoken understanding as they made their way down the familiar path. The moonlight cast long shadows over the gravestones, the only sound being their footsteps crunching on the gravel.

David led the way, his pace steady but with an underlying tension that Tyler could sense. It wasn't long before they arrived at a small, quaint house not far from the cemetery. The warm glow of lights shone through the windows, casting a halo around the house that seemed almost inviting.

Tyler paused a few steps behind David, taking in the sight. There was a certain serenity to the house, but Tyler could feel the weight of what it meant for David.

"This is it," David said quietly, stopping in front of the house. He turned to Tyler, a mixture of anticipation and nervousness etched across his face.

Tyler nodded, offering a reassuring smile. "I'll wait out here," he said gently. "I don't feel right looking in on her if I don't know her. But I'm here if you need me."

David looked relieved, giving Tyler a grateful nod. "Thanks, Tyler. I appreciate it."

Tyler watched as David approached the front door, his steps slow and deliberate. There was a moment of hesitation, and then David passed through the door, disappearing from Tyler's sight.

Tyler stood there, the cool night air wrapping around him as he kept his eyes on the house. He could feel the emotions swirling in the air—David's longing, his uncertainty, and the hope that maybe, just maybe, this would give him some closure.

Tyler waited patiently, his mind wandering to his own family, the time he had spent watching over them. He understood David's need, the pull to check in on those who had meant so much to him in life. It was a desire they both shared, a connection that kept them tethered to the world they once knew.

As the minutes ticked by, Tyler stayed where he was, a silent guardian standing vigil, ready to support his friend in whatever way he could.

Tyler stood by the window, his gaze fixed on the house. The soft, golden light from within cast fleeting shadows on the curtains, offering occasional glimpses of movement. He saw the woman David had spoken about pass by, her figure momentarily illuminated by the warm light. There was something about her that seemed oddly familiar, but Tyler couldn't quite place it. He shook off the thought, focusing instead on supporting his friend.

After a while, David emerged from the house, a profound look of relief and elation on his face. He walked with a lighter step, a stark contrast to the weight he had carried before.

Tyler approached him, concern etched in his features. "How did it go?" he asked, his voice gentle.

David's face broke into a relieved smile. "She went to my funeral," he said, his voice trembling with emotion. "I saw a card with my picture and the date of my funeral on it. She cared! She really did."

Tyler could see the joy and surprise in David's eyes, the weight of unspoken feelings finally lifting. "That's wonderful," Tyler said, sharing in David's relief. "It sounds like she truly valued you."

David nodded, his expression a mixture of happiness and wistfulness. "It means a lot to know that she did. I always wondered if she'd ever know how I felt, and now I know she did."

Tyler patted David on the back, offering a comforting gesture. "I'm glad you got that sense of closure," he said sincerely. "It's important to know that the people we care about are aware of our feelings, even if we can't always share them in person."

David looked at Tyler with gratitude. "Thanks for being here, Tyler. I couldn't have done this without your support."

Tyler smiled, understanding the depth of David's appreciation. "Anytime, David. I'm here for you."

With that, they turned and walked back towards the cemetery, the night air now feeling a bit lighter. David's steps were more buoyant, his heart a little lighter with the knowledge that his feelings had reached the woman he had cared about. Tyler followed, content in knowing he had helped his friend find some measure of peace.

As they walked back to the cemetery, the night air felt cooler, carrying a sense of calm after the emotional visit. Tyler glanced over at David, a question forming in his mind. "So, what's the girl's name?" he asked, curious.

David hesitated for a moment, then said, "This is going to sound weird, but I only know her as Nurse Jefferson. She works at the hospital where my mom has been staying on and off for a while. I got to know her pretty well during my visits, but I never had the courage to ask her out or find out her first name."

Tyler nodded thoughtfully. "It sounds like you had a special connection with her, even if you didn't get a chance to take it further."

David sighed, a touch of regret in his voice. "Yeah, it's strange. I knew her as Nurse Jefferson, and that's how she's known to me. It's a little frustrating not knowing more about her, especially now."

Tyler placed a reassuring hand on David's shoulder. "It's understandable to feel that way. Sometimes the connections we make are meaningful, even if they're incomplete. What matters is that you were able to find out that she cared about you."

David smiled, a sense of closure evident in his eyes. "You're right. Knowing that she cared, even if I didn't know her first name, means a lot."

Tyler nodded, appreciating the moment of clarity and understanding. "It's all part of finding peace and moving forward. We hold onto the good memories and the connections that mattered."

With a final glance at the cemetery, the two friends continued their walk back to their respective rooms, carrying with them the weight of their experiences and the small victories of the evening.

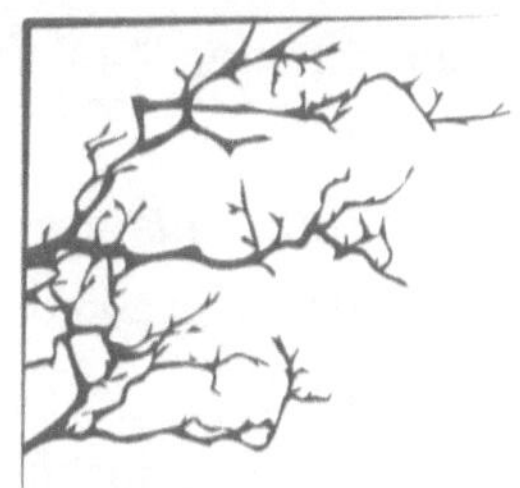

Chapter 11

Crossing the Threshold

TYLER WALKED THROUGH the quiet cemetery, the air thick with the scent of damp earth and the faint rustling of leaves. As he meandered between the gravestones, he came across one that bore a name familiar to him: Thomas Reed. He paused for a moment, contemplating, before raising his hand and gently knocking on the wooden door embedded in the stone.

"Come in," came the deep, familiar voice from inside.

Tyler pushed the door open and stepped inside, immediately greeted by the warmth of a crackling fireplace. The room was simple, yet it exuded a sense of comfort and history. The walls were made of rough-hewn wood, their dark grain polished with age, giving the space a cozy, cabin-like feel. An old armchair sat near the fire, its upholstery faded but well cared for, while a small wooden table held a few personal trinkets and a half-empty cup of tea.

Thomas sat in another chair by the fire, a blanket draped over his lap, his eyes twinkling as he looked up at Tyler. The room's simplicity, with its warm, earthy tones and the steady glow of the fire, seemed a perfect reflection of the man who lived here—steady, grounded, and at peace.

"Welcome, Tyler," Thomas said, his voice calm and inviting. "Take a seat, won't you? The fire's good company on a day like this."

Thomas looked at Tyler with an understanding smile, his eyes reflecting the warmth of the fire. "What can I help you with?" he asked, his voice gentle and full of the wisdom that came with age.

Tyler smiled back, feeling a deep sense of gratitude well up inside him. "For once, I just came to say thank you," he began, his voice steady. "Thank you for everything. You've helped me more than you know. I feel like I'm at total peace now, and without you, I wouldn't be where I'm at."

Thomas nodded slowly, his expression filled with quiet pride. "I'm glad to hear that, Tyler. You've come a long way, and I'm honored to have been part of your journey." He paused, letting the moment settle between them, the crackling of the fire the only sound in the room. "But remember, the peace you've found—it's within you. You've earned it."

Tyler felt a wave of emotion wash over him, a mix of relief and contentment. "I wouldn't have realized that without your guidance," he admitted. "You showed me the way, and I'll always be grateful for that."

Thomas reached out, placing a comforting hand on Tyler's shoulder. "You've done the hard work, Tyler. I'm proud of you."

Thomas's hand remained firm on Tyler's shoulder as he looked into his eyes with a seriousness that made the room feel even more still. "Just promise me one thing," Thomas said, his voice filled with a quiet intensity. "Promise me you won't ever give up. You're still there, Tyler. You still have life in you."

Tyler felt the weight of those words, a truth he hadn't fully accepted until now. He nodded slowly, understanding what Thomas was really saying. "I promise," Tyler replied, his voice steady. "I won't give up."

Thomas's expression softened, a hint of relief crossing his features. "Good," he said, giving Tyler's shoulder a reassuring squeeze. "That's all I needed to hear."

Tyler felt a sense of determination rise within him, a renewed purpose. He knew now that his journey wasn't over—there was still more ahead, and he was ready to face it.

Tyler gave Thomas one last, grateful smile before turning toward the door. "I'm going back to my room," he said, his voice calm yet resolute. "Thank you again, for everything."

Thomas nodded, understanding the depth of Tyler's words. "Anytime, Tyler. Remember, you're not alone."

Tyler left the warm glow of Thomas's room and walked back through the cemetery, his steps more certain than they'd ever been. The gravestones seemed to stand taller, their inscriptions clearer as he passed. When he reached his own door, he paused for a moment, taking in the words etched there.

He opened the door and stepped into his room. The familiar living room greeted him, everything in its place—the cozy furniture, the warm lighting—but it felt incomplete without Jessica there. Yet, despite the emptiness, Tyler felt a profound sense of peace. He had made his decision. He was ready for whatever came next.

Tyler lowered himself onto the floor, the plush carpet cushioning him as he sat cross-legged in the center of the room. He closed his eyes, letting the quiet of the space wash over him. He focused on his breathing, slow and steady—inhale, exhale. Each breath filled him with a calm that settled deep within his chest.

But as he breathed, the words of Thomas echoed in his mind, persistent and clear: "You still have life. Don't ever give up."

The phrase repeated itself with every inhale and exhale, weaving through his thoughts like a thread pulling everything together. Tyler's mind drifted back to his family, to the life he once lived, and the life he still might have.

With each breath, the room around him seemed to fade, and the image of his family grew stronger in his mind. He could see Jessica's smile, hear Oliver's laughter, feel Grace's tiny hand in his. The more he focused on them, the more real they felt, as if they were within reach.

Tyler opened his eyes slowly, the room coming back into focus, but the words remained with him, stronger now: "You still have life."

Tyler let himself sink deeper into the peace that enveloped him, the love he held for his family filling every corner of his being. The bond with David, the friendships he had forged, all came together in a comforting warmth that spread throughout him. With his eyes still closed, he felt a strange sensation, as if something unseen was lifting him from the floor.

It wasn't just a physical feeling—it was something more profound. He felt lighter, as if the burdens he'd carried since the accident were slowly being lifted away, one by one. The love and peace he had found within himself seemed to radiate outward, surrounding him in an ethereal glow.

The sensation grew stronger, and for a moment, he wasn't sure if he was still sitting on the floor or floating in the air. It didn't matter. He was being guided by something greater than himself, something that understood his journey and where it was meant to lead.

Tyler opened his eyes to find a large, glowing orb of light hovering before him. Its radiant glow filled the room, casting everything in a warm, otherworldly hue. He had heard of this light before—a guiding force that appeared when a soul was ready to move on to its final resting place.

His heart raced with a mix of emotions: fear, curiosity, and a profound sense of peace. Was this truly his time? Would stepping into that light mean leaving everything behind forever? Would he ever see his family again if he took this step?

The questions swirled in his mind, but deep down, Tyler knew that this light had appeared because he had found peace within himself. The love he had for his family, the bonds he had formed, and the closure he had achieved had all led him to this moment.

He wasn't sure what lay ahead, but he knew that whatever it was, it would be a continuation of his journey. The peace he had found gave him the courage to take the chance, to trust that this light would lead him to where he was meant to be.

With a deep breath, Tyler took a step forward, moving closer to the orb. The light seemed to pulse in response, as if welcoming him. He hesitated for only a moment, thinking of Jessica, Oliver, and Grace. But in his heart, he felt a reassurance that this wasn't the end—it was just another step in his journey.

And with that, Tyler stepped into the light, embracing whatever came next.

Tyler stood at the threshold of the brilliant light, its radiance enveloping him in a warmth that felt both familiar and new. It wasn't like the cold, detached brightness he had feared before; this light was different—gentle, almost inviting. But as he lingered there, something inside him stirred—a pull, subtle at first, like a whisper, urging him to retreat, to go back to the room that had been his sanctuary.

For a moment, the pull grew stronger, tempting him with the comfort of the known, the room where he had found peace. But deep within, Tyler felt an inexplicable urge to move forward. The light called to him, not with promises of peace or finality, but with a sense of purpose, of something unfinished.

He hesitated, his heart torn between the pull of the familiar and the unknown path ahead. Then, as he stood there, the voices of those who had guided him began to fill the space around him, each one urging him forward.

"You still have life in you. Don't ever give up," Thomas's words echoed in his mind, grounding him in the resolve he had found with the old man's guidance.

"You are my everything, more than you know," his own voice, filled with love and regret, reminded him of the family he couldn't leave behind.

"You've got this," Clara's encouraging words floated through the light, a reminder of the strength he had found in himself.

The pull from the room behind him persisted, trying to lure him back, but Tyler focused on the voices, the words that had shaped his journey. He knew he couldn't go back—not now, not when he had come this far. The light, though unknown, felt right, like a path he was meant to take.

With every step he took toward the light, the pull from behind lessened, replaced by a growing sense of clarity. The warmth of the light surrounded him, not as an end, but as a new beginning. Tyler could feel the weight of the world lifting from his shoulders, replaced by a lightness that filled him with hope.

He kept moving forward, each step more confident than the last. The voices grew softer, not fading, but merging with the light, becoming a part of it. They weren't gone; they were with him, guiding him through the brightness that now seemed less blinding and more welcoming.

Tyler took a deep breath, feeling the light fill him, energize him. He didn't know what lay ahead, but he knew it was right. The force pulling him back had all but disappeared, replaced by a forward momentum that he couldn't resist. The light was his path, and he was ready to follow it.

As Tyler neared the end of the light, a sudden force yanked at him with a ferocity he hadn't felt before. It was as if something, or someone, was trying to pull him back, to drag him away from the light that had filled him with such hope. The pull was strong—almost overwhelming—threatening to undo all the progress he had made.

He didn't understand what was happening, but a deep, instinctual part of him knew that he couldn't let it win. This was his fight now, and he couldn't let go. The voices of Thomas, Clara, and his family echoed in his mind, giving him strength, urging him forward even as the pull threatened to tear him apart.

Gritting his teeth, Tyler mustered every ounce of strength he had left. His heart pounded in his chest as he pushed against the force, refusing to be dragged back. The light was so close—he could feel it, taste it, almost touch it. With a surge of determination, Tyler broke into a run, propelling himself toward the end of the light, refusing to let the darkness win.

He ran with everything he had, his legs moving faster and faster, the pull behind him growing weaker with each step. The light around him began to blur as he sprinted toward the end, and just as he felt the pull begin to wane, the light ahead of him suddenly disappeared. He was plunged into darkness—total, consuming darkness.

For a moment, there was nothing. No light, no sound, no pull—just an overwhelming sensation of weightlessness. Tyler floated in the void, unsure of where he was or what had just happened. The world around him was dark and silent, but instead of fear, he felt a strange sense of calm.

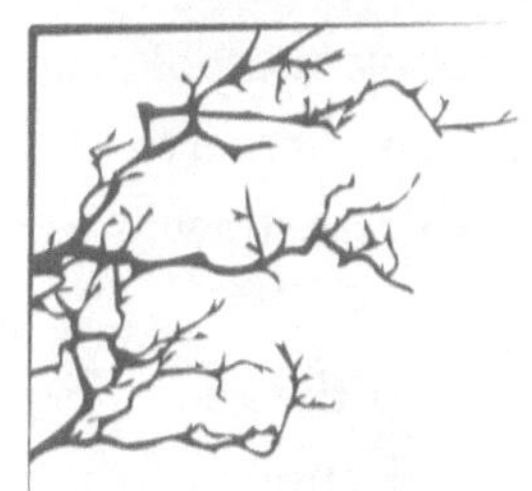

Chapter 12

A Special Place

Tyler struggled to open his eyes, his body feeling heavy as if it had been weighed down by years of stillness. He tried to move, but everything felt distant, almost foreign. Instinctively, he reached out with his hands, trying to grasp something familiar. His fingers brushed against the fabric of a blanket beneath him, and then he felt it—a warm, comforting touch.

A hand, gentle and familiar, held his. The sensation was both grounding and overwhelming, flooding him with memories and emotions. With a tremendous effort, Tyler pried his eyes open, the world around him slowly coming into focus.

The first thing he saw was Jessica. Her face was pale, her eyes red and swollen with tears, but the moment their gazes met, her expression shifted. Relief, love, and disbelief mingled in her features as tears streamed down her face. She squeezed his hand tighter, as if afraid he might slip away again.

"Tyler..." she whispered, her voice trembling with emotion. The sound of her voice, so real and close, filled him with a warmth that was more powerful than anything he had felt in his long journey.

He tried to speak, but his throat was dry, and all that came out was a faint, rasping breath. But it didn't matter—Jessica was there, and that was enough.

Tyler heard a gentle knock at the door, breaking the poignant moment between him and Jessica. She looked up, her eyes still shimmering with tears. "Come in," she said, her voice betraying her fragile emotional state.

The door creaked open, and a nurse stepped into the room, her presence both professional and comforting. She had an air of calm assurance about her, which Tyler found soothing amidst the whirlwind of his returning senses.

"Hi, Tyler," she said with a warm smile. "I'm Nurse Jefferson. I'm glad to see you're awake. You've been in a coma for quite some time, but it's wonderful to see you here now." She reached out and gently touched Tyler's arm, offering a reassuring squeeze. "I'm here to help in any way I can. The doctor will be along shortly to check on you."

Tyler managed a faint nod, his mind still reeling from the transition from his ethereal journey to this stark, new reality. He glanced at Jessica, who looked between him and the nurse, her expression a mixture of relief and lingering anxiety.

"Thank you," Tyler croaked, his voice barely more than a whisper. The effort of speaking felt monumental, but he was determined to connect, to bridge the gap between the world he had just left and the one he was re-entering.

Nurse Jefferson gave a comforting nod. "Take your time, Tyler. You've been through a lot, and we'll take it one step at a time. Just rest for now, and we'll get everything sorted out."

Jessica remained by Tyler's side, her hand still holding his, her presence a grounding anchor as they awaited the doctor's arrival.

There was another knock at the door, and Jessica, still holding Tyler's hand, responded, "Come in."

The door opened, and a figure walked in, his presence exuding a blend of authority and empathy. Tyler struggled to focus his blurry vision, his eyes not yet fully adjusting to the light. The figure came closer, and Tyler could make out the distinct features of the man—a calm, reassuring demeanor paired with a gentle smile.

"Hello, Tyler," the man said, his voice carrying a soothing resonance. "I'm Dr. Thomas Reed. Both Ms. Jefferson and I have been looking after you for the past few months."

The name struck Tyler like a jolt of electricity. Thomas Reed? The same name as the Civil War veteran he had spoken to in his afterlife journey? He struggled to process this coincidence or, perhaps, a sign.

His voice, though weak, managed to croak out, "Thomas Reed? Jefferson? This can't be..."

Dr. Reed's eyes softened as he saw the confusion in Tyler's gaze. "I understand this must be overwhelming," he said gently. "It's a lot to take in. But I assure you, you're in good hands. Your journey back to the world of the living is a significant step, and we're here to support you every step of the way."

Jessica, her eyes wide with surprise, glanced between Tyler and Dr. Reed, sensing the depth of this unexpected connection. She squeezed Tyler's hand reassuringly, offering her silent support as the doctor continued.

"We'll take things slowly," Dr. Reed continued, his voice calm and steady. "I'll perform a thorough examination to ensure everything is as it should be. You've been through a lot, and we're here to help you adjust."

As Dr. Reed approached Tyler's bedside, Tyler's mind raced, trying to reconcile the reality of the doctor before him with the ethereal presence he had encountered. This was a new chapter, one filled with both hope and uncertainty, but the familiar warmth of Jessica's hand and the reassuring presence of Dr. Reed promised that he was not alone in this transition back to life.

Jessica looked at Dr. Reed and asked, "Do you mind?" while gesturing toward the door.

"Of course," Dr. Reed replied, understanding her wish for privacy.

Jessica quietly walked to the door and opened it. Tyler's vision was gradually sharpening, and as he focused, he saw Jessica guide Oliver and Grace toward his bedside. The sight brought a rush of emotions to Tyler. Tears began streaming down his face as he felt the gentle, familiar touches of his children's small hands on his arm.

Grace, with her wide, innocent eyes, looked up at the nurse and said, "Hey, Miss Jefferson."

Tyler's heart ached with a mix of overwhelming love and relief as he saw his children standing before him. The room seemed to warm with their presence, filling the space with a sense of normalcy and profound connection. Jessica's eyes were misty with tears as she watched her children's interaction with Tyler, her own hand squeezing his as she witnessed the reunion.

Dr. Reed, standing by the door, gave the family a moment of privacy, knowing how crucial this moment was for their emotional healing. He watched with a compassionate gaze as the family came together, realizing the importance of these first, tender moments of reconnection.

As Tyler lay there, surrounded by his family, a realization began to dawn on him. The experiences he had during his coma—the cemetery, the people he met, the conversations—had all been fragments of reality, overheard and woven into his unconscious mind.

His thoughts turned to David, his friend who had been with him in that strange, dreamlike world. Summoning what little strength he had, Tyler managed to whisper, "David?"

Jessica, sitting close by, leaned in to hear him better. Her expression softened, and she gently squeezed his hand. "He passed on impact, Tyler," she said, her voice tinged with sorrow. "I'm so sorry."

Tyler's heart sank as the words confirmed what he had feared. David hadn't made it. The connection they'd shared in that other place had been real in a sense, but now Tyler was left with the painful truth that his friend was gone.

Tyler's gaze drifted to the corner beside his bed, where a collection of flowers had been carefully arranged, brought by family and friends who had kept vigil during his coma. Each bouquet was a testament to their love and hope, but one card in particular caught his eye.

With great effort, he reached over and managed to grab the card, his fingers trembling slightly. As he turned it over, he saw Jessica's familiar handwriting. The simple words, "From Jessica," were written on one side, but when he flipped it, he found a message that made his heart swell: "Remember our special place."

He looked up at Jessica, who was sitting by his side, her eyes filled with emotion. "I will never forget that," Tyler whispered, his voice raspy but full of meaning. The memory of their special place, a symbol of their love and connection, was something that had sustained him even in the darkest of times.

Jessica smiled through her tears, leaning in to gently kiss his forehead. "I know you won't," she whispered back, her voice full of love.

He managed a weak smile, his throat dry as he tried to speak. "How...how long?"

"Three months," Jessica said, her voice steady despite the emotions brimming beneath the surface. "You've been in a coma for three months."

Tyler's heart sank at the thought of all he had missed. Oliver and Grace stood by the bed, their expressions a mix of relief and uncertainty.

"How have the kids taken this?" He asks.

Jessica squeezed his hand reassuringly. "They're doing okay. Oliver's been keeping up with school and trying to make everyone laugh, just like always. Grace...she's been quieter, but she's strong. They've missed you so much, Tyler. We all have."

Tyler reached out with his other hand, managing to brush his fingers against Oliver's hair and then Grace's cheek. "I missed you too, buddy. And you, sweetie."

Grace leaned in, pressing her small hand against his. "Daddy, we've been waiting for you to wake up."

"I'm here now," Tyler whispered, his heart full as he looked at his children. "I'm here."

He turned to the other side of the bed where nurse Jefferson was taking his vitals.

Tyler's eyes narrowed slightly as he studied her face, something about her seemed familiar. Then, it clicked. "Nurse Jefferson...is your name Carla?"

She blinked in surprise, then nodded. "Yes, it is. How did you know?"

Tyler's heart quickened as memories from his time in the coma began to surface. "Did you know a man named David? He used to visit the hospital a lot...for his mother."

Carla's expression softened, and she nodded. "Yes, I did. David was a wonderful person. He visited often, and over time, we became friends. He always talked about asking someone out...he was a good man."

Tyler swallowed hard, emotions welling up inside him. "He...he cared about you. More than you know."

Carla's eyes glistened as she nodded slowly. "I cared about him too. I'm sorry to hear he's gone."

Tyler looked at Jessica, then back at Carla, feeling the weight of everything that had happened in those three months. "Thank you, Carla...for everything."

Carla smiled gently, placing a comforting hand on his arm. "You're welcome, Tyler. Take your time. You've been through a lot, but you're here now, and that's what matters."

As she left the room, Tyler turned back to his family, his heart full. He knew that someday, he would tell Jessica and the kids everything about what he had experienced. But for now, he was content to simply be with them, grateful to be back in their lives.

Jessica looked at Tyler, her eyes filled with warmth and relief. "We've been by your side every day," she began, her voice emotional but steady. "The kids would sit here, and I'd read to them, just to keep the room full of life. We read so many stories, hoping you could hear us somehow."

Tyler listened, a swell of emotions rising within him as he imagined the scenes she described.

"Your parents came a lot too," Jessica continued. "They were so worried about you. It was hard for them to see you like this, but they never gave up hope."

Tyler's heart ached at the thought of his parents, their unwavering love and concern. He wished he could have told them then how much he appreciated their presence, how much it meant to him.

"And," Jessica added with a small smile, "the doctor even let Scout come in for a little bit. She was so excited to see you, she started barking like crazy. We had to take her out, but for a moment, it felt like everything was normal again."

Tyler chuckled softly, the sound of Scout's bark echoing in his memory. "I can picture that," he said, his voice still weak but growing stronger with every word.

As Jessica continued to speak, Tyler's mind drifted back to everything he had seen and heard during those long months. The way he had perceived the events in his mind—the visits, the stories, the conversations—had been so vivid, so real. Yet, here was Jessica, recounting the same moments from a different perspective. It was as if his mind had taken the fragments of their world and reassembled them into something familiar but altogether different.

He remembered the times he had felt their presence, the moments when he thought he heard their voices or felt their touch. Now, it all began to make sense—how his mind had woven the reality of their visits into the dreamlike experiences he'd had while in the coma.

"I remember," Tyler said quietly, his eyes meeting Jessica's. "I remember hearing your voice, feeling you all there with me. It was different, but I knew you were close. That's what kept me going."

Jessica squeezed his hand, her eyes glistening with tears. "We were never going to give up on you, Tyler. Not for a second."

Tyler nodded, overwhelmed by the love and support that had surrounded him, even when he couldn't fully understand it. He looked at his children, then back at Jessica, his heart full. "Thank you," he whispered. "Thank you for everything."

As Tyler lay there, still trying to grasp the full weight of his awakening, the door to his room opened once more. His parents rushed in, their faces a mixture of disbelief and overwhelming joy.

His mother was the first to reach him, her tears already flowing freely. She cradled his face in her hands, her touch trembling with emotion. "Oh, Tyler," she whispered, her voice thick with tears. "I can't believe it. You're really awake."

Tyler looked into his mother's eyes, seeing the months of worry and fear melt away, replaced by pure elation. "I'm here, Mom," he said shakily, his own eyes welling up. "I'm here."

His father, usually so stoic and composed, followed close behind. For a moment, he simply stood there, staring at Tyler as if he were a miracle. The brave face he always wore had been replaced with a raw, unguarded expression of pure joy. Finally, unable to hold back any longer, he stepped forward and grasped Tyler's hand, his grip firm yet tender.

"Son," his father choked out, his voice breaking with emotion. "You don't know how long we've waited for this moment."

Tyler squeezed his father's hand in return, feeling the strength and love in that simple gesture. "I'm sorry I worried you," Tyler said, his voice thick with emotion. "I'm so sorry."

His father shook his head, blinking back tears. "Don't you dare apologize, Tyler. You've come back to us, and that's all that matters."

The room was filled with the quiet sounds of their reunion—his mother's sobs of relief, his father's whispered words of gratitude, Jessica's gentle touch as she watched the scene unfold. Tyler felt the warmth of their love envelop him, stronger than ever before.

For a moment, the world outside the hospital room faded away, leaving only the profound sense of connection and love that had sustained them all through the darkest of times. Tyler realized then just how deep their bond truly was, how much his family meant to him, and how much he meant to them.

After a while, Jessica gathered the kids, and with a loving smile, she leaned in to kiss Tyler's forehead. "We'll be right back, okay? Just going to walk your parents to the car," she said. Tyler nodded, watching as they all left the room, their voices fading as they made their way down the hall.

The room fell silent, save for the rhythmic beeping of the heart monitor. Tyler closed his eyes for a moment, letting the quietness of the space sink in. He was still adjusting to the reality of being awake, of being back.

A gentle knock at the door brought him out of his thoughts. "Come in," Tyler called out, his voice still hoarse.

The door opened, and Dr. Thomas Reed stepped in, his presence calm and reassuring. "Hello, Tyler," Dr. Reed greeted him with a warm smile. "How are you feeling?"

Tyler took a deep breath, considering the question. "I'm... better. Tired, but better," he replied honestly.

Dr. Reed nodded, stepping closer to the bed to check the monitors. "That's to be expected. You've been through quite an ordeal."

Tyler watched him work for a moment, gathering his thoughts. "Doctor, I wanted to tell you something," he began. "While I was... under, I guess... I heard you. A lot, actually. Your voice, your words. They kept me going, in a way."

Dr. Reed paused, looking at Tyler with a mixture of surprise and curiosity. "You heard me?" he asked, his tone gentle.

Tyler nodded. "I don't remember everything clearly, but I remember your voice. You told me not to give up, that I still had life in me. It was like... like you were there with me, even though I was somewhere else entirely."

A soft smile touched Dr. Reed's lips. "I'm glad my words reached you, Tyler. Sometimes, when a patient is in a coma, we talk to them, hoping they might hear us. It seems like, in your case, those words found their way to you."

Tyler felt a wave of gratitude wash over him. "Thank you, Dr. Reed. For everything. I can't even begin to express how much it means to me that you were there, looking after me, helping me find my way back."

Dr. Reed placed a reassuring hand on Tyler's shoulder. "You did the hard work, Tyler. You found the strength within yourself to come back. But I'm honored to have been a part of your journey."

Tyler looked into Dr. Reed's eyes and saw the genuine care and compassion that had guided him through this experience. "I won't forget it," Tyler said, his voice full of sincerity. "I won't forget any of it."

Dr. Reed gave him a nod, his expression one of quiet pride. "And I won't forget you, Tyler. Now, rest up. You have a lot of living to do."

With that, Dr. Reed gave Tyler one last, encouraging smile before making his way to the door. Tyler watched him leave, feeling an overwhelming sense of peace settle over him. He had fought his way back to life, and with the help of those who cared for him, he was ready to embrace it fully.

As Jessica and the kids returned to the room, Tyler felt a rush of joy. The room, now filled with the warm presence of his family, was a place of comfort and familiarity. Grace and Oliver, full of energy and excitement, took their places at the foot of Tyler's bed. Jessica settled in a chair beside him, ready to continue a cherished tradition.

"Now how about a story?" Tyler suggested, his voice filled with affection.

Grace's eyes lit up. "Felix!" she exclaimed, her enthusiasm infectious.

Tyler chuckled. "Ah, Felix. That's a story I know very well."

"Once upon a time," Tyler started, his eyes twinkling, "there was a clever little fox named Felix. Felix lived in a cozy den at the edge of a vast and enchanted forest. He was known far and wide for his curiosity and bravery."

Grace and Oliver leaned in, their eyes wide with interest.

"One sunny morning," Tyler continued, "Felix set out on a new adventure. He had heard tales of a magical meadow where the flowers sparkled like stars and the river sang the sweetest songs. With his little red tail twitching with excitement, Felix trotted through the forest, eager to see this wonder for himself."

Tyler described the journey with vivid imagery, just as he had heard Jessica narrate it. The dense forest with its towering trees, the dappled sunlight filtering through the leaves, and the soft rustling of the underbrush created a vivid scene in the room.

"As Felix ventured deeper into the forest," Tyler's voice carried a note of wonder, "he came across a wise old owl perched on a branch. The owl told Felix that the magical meadow was not just a place but a state of mind—one where you could find beauty and joy if you looked with an open heart."

The children listened intently, absorbed in the story. Tyler continued, his voice gentle and soothing, recounting how Felix faced challenges and made new friends along his journey. The story mirrored the one he had witnessed Jessica telling them, with its gentle moral about the importance of kindness and courage.

"When Felix finally reached the magical meadow," Tyler said, "he found it to be more magnificent than he had ever imagined. The flowers glowed with a light, and the river's song filled the air with a melody of peace and happiness. Felix realized that the true magic was in the journey he had taken and the friends he had made along the way."

As he finished the story, Tyler looked at Jessica and the kids with a contented smile. The room, now filled with the echoes of the bedtime tale, seemed to wrap them all in a cocoon of warmth and love. Tyler felt a profound sense of gratitude for these simple yet precious moments, knowing that the love he had always cherished was now a tangible part of his life again.

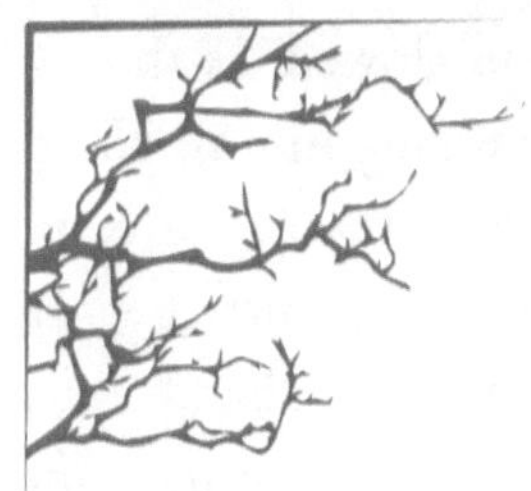

Chapter 13

Epitaph of Peace

THE AIR WAS DENSE WITH the weight of a thousand whispered secrets as Tyler Lawson made his way through the ancient cemetery, where time itself seemed to have slowed its relentless march. The sky, a vault of heavy, brooding clouds, cast an ashen pallor over the landscape, muting the colors of the world until all that remained was a dismal shade of gray. The autumn chill had settled into the earth, and with each step Tyler took, the crisp leaves beneath his feet surrendered their brittle bodies to the cold, echoing the sound of his passage with a hollow, mournful crunch.

A breeze, gentle yet insistent, wound its way through the gnarled branches of the trees that stood as silent sentinels over the resting places of the departed. It whispered through the boughs, a voice without a source, carrying with it the faintest scent of damp earth and the decaying remnants of the season. Tyler drew in a breath, tasting the cold on his tongue, a sharp tang that seemed to chill him from the inside out. The air was so still, so laden with the promise of coming frost, that even the distant calls of the birds were muted, their cries swallowed by the oppressive undertone.

As he approached David's grave, Tyler's steps slowed, as though some unseen force had taken hold of his limbs, urging him to pause, to reflect. The headstone, a simple and unadorned marker of a life now extinguished, rose from the earth like a sentinel, its surface worn smooth by the relentless passage of time. With a trembling hand, Tyler reached out, his fingers brushing the cold, unyielding stone. The sensation sent a shiver coursing through his body, not from the chill, but from the flood of memories that surged forth, unbidden, from the depths of his mind.

The cemetery, in its solemn silence, seemed to close in around him, the graves stretching out in all directions like the ripples on a pond, each one a reminder of the countless souls who had come before. The trees, their leaves clinging desperately to their branches, seemed to lean in, as though listening for the words that hung unspoken in the air. The wind picked up, a low moan that swirled around him, tugging at his coat, urging him to speak, to give voice to the thoughts that churned within him.

But Tyler remained silent, his gaze fixed on the name etched into the stone before him. He could feel the weight of the world pressing down on him, a crushing reminder of all that had been lost, of all that could never be reclaimed. The stillness of the place was almost suffocating, as though the very earth itself was holding its breath, waiting for something—anything—to break the silence.

And yet, despite the repressive gloom, there was a strange sense of peace here, a quiet acceptance that settled over Tyler like a shroud. The cold that bit at his skin, the scent of decay that lingered in the air, the muted light that bathed the cemetery in its ghostly glow—all of it seemed to speak of an ending, but also of a beginning. For in this place, where the living and the dead existed side by side, there was the faintest glimmer of hope, a whisper of something more, something beyond the cold embrace of the grave.

He knelt, his knees sinking into the wet soil, and traced the engraved letters of David's name with a trembling finger. The silence was profound, broken only by the occasional chirp of a bird, unaware of the solemnity of the moment.

"David," Tyler began, his voice barely more than a whisper, carried away by the breeze that swirled through the cemetery. "I wanted to thank you—for everything you did for me. I'm standing here today because of you, because of the peace you helped me find."

He paused, letting his words settle into the stillness around him, as if waiting for a response from beyond the grave. The wind picked up slightly, rustling the leaves above, and he could almost imagine it was David, listening.

"I met her, David," Tyler continued, his voice gaining strength. "Nurse Jefferson—Carla. She did attend your funeral, just like you hoped. She cares for people deeply, just like you thought. I could see it in her eyes. She spoke about you with such warmth... It was as if a part of you lived on in her."

"She even said she missed her sister's wedding to attend." He continued.

The clouds above shifted, casting fleeting shadows across the headstones, and Tyler felt a pang of sorrow, mingled with gratitude. He pressed his hand against the cold granite, feeling the rough texture beneath his palm, grounding himself in the reality of the moment.

"You were right about her," he said. "And I think... I think she would have said yes, David. If you had asked her out, I think she would have said yes."

Tyler's voice cracked slightly as he spoke, the weight of his emotions pressing down on him, yet there was a clarity in his heart that he hadn't felt before. The truth of what had been lost and the beauty of what had been preserved intertwined in his mind, forming a bittersweet melody that resonated within him.

"You helped me find my way back," Tyler whispered, bowing his head. "And for that, I'll be forever grateful. I hope you've found peace, wherever you are."

Tyler lingered for a moment longer, the weight of his words still hanging in the crisp morning air. The world around him felt eerily still, as if it too were holding its breath, waiting for something unspoken. With a slow, deliberate motion, he reached into his coat pocket and pulled out a small piece of folded parchment. The edges were slightly frayed, and the ink had smudged in places from where his trembling hand had held it too tightly.

He stared at the note for a long time, the words he had written in the solitude of his room now carrying a gravity that he hadn't fully anticipated. It was a simple message, but one that encapsulated everything he wanted to say, everything he had felt in the days since waking from his long slumber. With a sigh, he knelt down again, pressing the note gently against the base of the headstone, where it would be sheltered from the elements.

The cold, unyielding stone was a stark contrast to the warmth he felt in his heart, a warmth that had been rekindled through the memories of his time with David, both in life and in that strange, liminal space between worlds. Tyler placed his hand on the grave one last time, a final goodbye to the friend who had guided him through the darkness.

As he stood up, the wind swirled around him, picking up stray leaves and sending them dancing through the air. He closed his eyes and let the breeze wash over him, a cleansing force that seemed to carry away the remnants of his sorrow. He turned slowly, his footsteps crunching on the gravel path as he began to walk away.

Each step felt like a release, a shedding of the past as he moved forward into whatever lay ahead. The trees whispered, their branches swaying as if to bid him farewell. The scent of earth and rain filled his senses, grounding him in the present, in the here and now.

Tyler didn't look back as he walked, but the cemetery seemed to fade behind him, the figures of the gravestones blending into the mist that rolled in from the hills. He felt lighter, more at peace than he had in a long time, and as he approached the gate, he knew that something had shifted within him—a final, irreversible change.

Just as he reached the iron gate, the note he had left behind caught the breeze, fluttering slightly against the stone. It was a small, unassuming piece of paper, but it held a message that resonated deeply. The words he had written, in his careful, deliberate hand, were a reminder, a promise, a hope for something more.

The note lay quiet, a silent testament to the bond between two souls who had crossed paths in the most unlikely of circumstances. And on that note, in the final line, were the words:

"Remember your special place."

Don't miss out!

Visit the website below and you can sign up to receive emails whenever K.E.W. publishes a new book. There's no charge and no obligation.

https://books2read.com/r/B-A-RJUBB-FJSRE

BOOKS 2 READ

Connecting independent readers to independent writers.

Did you love *Room Below The World*? Then you should read *The Pineworth Chronicles*[1] by K.E.W.!

[2]

"The Pineworth Chronicles," a compelling series that delves into the challenges and sacrifices faced by first responders. In this gripping collection, readers will be immersed in the demanding world of emergency services, gaining a profound understanding of the trials and triumphs these heroes encounter.Book 1: "The Crossroads of Duty" explores the complex decisions that first responders confront in critical moments. Join our protagonists as they navigate the ethical dilemmas that arise when duty clashes with personal beliefs, witnessing the profound impact these choices have on their lives and the lives of those they serve.Book 2: "The Often Forgotten Hero" shines a light on the unsung heroes of emergency services. Dive into the stories of

---

1. https://books2read.com/u/m26K2o

2. https://books2read.com/u/m26K2o

individuals who tirelessly work behind the scenes, providing crucial support and expertise. Discover the immense contributions made by these often overlooked figures and develop a newfound appreciation for their indispensable role in the first responder community.Book 3: "The Rookie's Journey" takes readers on an emotional rollercoaster as we follow a young and inexperienced first responder. Witness their transformation from a wide-eyed novice to a seasoned professional, as they navigate the intense physical and emotional challenges that come with the job. Experience their growth, resilience, and self-discovery throughout their journey.

Also by K.E.W.

The Pineworth Chronicles
The Crossroads Of Duty
The Often Forgotten Hero
A Rookie's Journey
Secrets Among The Stones
1971

Standalone
The Pineworth Chronicles
Room Below The World

About the Author

K.E.W. is the pseudonymous voice behind a budding literary journey, merging the worlds of law enforcement and storytelling. Having served within law enforcement since 2016, and as a dedicated school resource officer from 2021, K.E.W. draws inspiration from these experiences.Through their writing, K.E.W. seeks to illuminate the intricate struggles inherent in upholding the law while championing social justice reform. Their poignant narratives delve into these complexities, aiming to resonate particularly with the young minds frequenting the hallways of local public schools. K.E.W.'s published works offer thought-provoking insights and inspiring tales woven from the fabric of their unique career path.

About the Publisher

White Quill Writings was founded in 2023 on the shared passion for storytelling and literary expression, White Quill Writings is the brainchild of a devoted husband and wife duo. With a vision to empower authors and bring exceptional stories to life, they embarked on this self-publishing venture.

Driven by a commitment to support emerging voices and diverse narratives, White Quill Writings offers a platform that values creativity, authenticity, and individuality. Their dedication to nurturing writers shines through personalized guidance, professional editing, and tailored publishing solutions.

As a testament to their unwavering belief in the power of words, this partnership fosters a community where stories flourish, authors thrive, and dreams of publication become tangible realities. White Quill Writings stands as an inviting gateway for writers seeking to share their unique tales with the world.

Read more at https://instagram.com/whitequillwritings.